"I... Leo, I don'

"That's okay. Neither
again, this time to t

"I don't do affairs, either." The words came out
as a husky whisper.

"Neither do I." His eyes, too, had darkened.
And she noticed that they were fixed on her
mouth.

"But maybe we should," he continued. "Maybe
we should just have a wild, wild affair and get
this out of our systems."

"There's nothing to get out of my system."

He lifted an eyebrow. "Isn't there?"

MISTRESS ON TRIAL

KATE HARDY

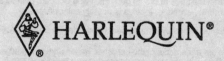

HARLEQUIN®

TORONTO • NEW YORK • LONDON
AMSTERDAM • PARIS • SYDNEY • HAMBURG
STOCKHOLM • ATHENS • TOKYO • MILAN • MADRID
PRAGUE • WARSAW • BUDAPEST • AUCKLAND

ISBN-13: 978-0-373-82054-2
ISBN-10:   0-373-82054-2

MISTRESS ON TRIAL

First North American Publication 2007.

Previously published in the U.K. under the title *Strictly Legal*.

www.eHarlequin.com

Printed in U.S.A.

MISTRESS ON TRIAL

For Cathy,
with love and thanks for all your
support and encouragement over the years.

CHAPTER ONE

'YOU look like a princess,' a sleepy voice murmured.

And she did. Like a gypsy princess. Barefoot, in a white slub-silk slip dress trimmed with lace, with a crimson feather boa draped round her shoulders, a sparkly tiara in her hair and dark curls corkscrewing down her back, she should have looked a mess. Like an adult playing at dressing up.

Instead, she looked good enough to eat.

And he could imagine her wearing *just* the feather boa...

Leo Ballantyne was furious with himself for thinking that way about Rose Carter—his baby sister's best friend and, in his view, the worst thing that had ever happened to Sara. Rose was bad news, with a capital B. And now Sara had gone off somewhere for a few days and left Rose—one of her flakiest, most unreliable friends—to look after Daisy.

Unbelievable.

So much for thinking that motherhood had settled Sara and made her more responsible; she still clearly had the 'wild child' streak she'd had since her teens, doing whatever she pleased and leaving everyone else to sort out the chaos she trailed in her wake.

And no way was Leo letting his four-year-old niece stay in the care of Rose Carter. Even if Rose *was* cuddling Daisy right now and reading her a story. Daisy should have been in bed and asleep ages ago. And the flat was a complete tip. The living room looked as if it had been burgled, with things strewn every-where and a huge pile of laundry just dumped on one of the chairs. He shuddered to think what the kitchen looked like. How could one woman make so much mess in the space of half a day?

Then Rose glanced up, saw him leaning against the doorjamb, and shrieked.

'It's all right, Aunty Rose, it's not a burglar. It's only Uncle Leo,' Daisy said as she peered round Rose. She gave Leo the wide smile that always melted his heart, and a tiny little wave. ''Lo, Uncle Leo.'

He smiled back. 'Hello, Princess.'

Rose stroked the little girl's hair. 'I'm sorry if I scared you when I screamed, Daze. I was just a bit surprised because I wasn't expecting to see anyone.' Her mouth thinned as she looked straight at Leo again. 'I didn't hear you knock.'

Because he hadn't bothered. He'd found out the situation from his mother; Sara's phone had switched to answering machine and her mobile phone had been turned off, so he'd driven straight over to Sara's flat to see for himself what the situation was and whether his niece was all right.

Right now, his worst fears had been realised.

He became aware that Rose was waiting for an answer. Why hadn't he knocked? 'I have Sara's spare key.'

'And you normally just let yourself in?'

Of course not. He had that key for emergencies—and, in his view, this counted as an emergency. Was Rose trying to make him feel guilty for looking after his little sister and his niece? 'This isn't a normal situation,' he said coolly.

Rose frowned at him. *'Pas devant l'enfant.'*

He blinked. Was it his imagination, or had she just spoken French to him in a perfect accent? He'd had no idea that she knew French. *Not in front of the child.* She was right. They shouldn't drag Daisy into this. And it riled him that she was the one who'd been responsible enough to think of it, not him.

'Go and make yourself a coffee or something. I'm reading Daisy a bedtime story. And then you're going to go to sleep, aren't you, sweetheart, while Uncle Leo and I have a little chat in the kitchen?'

'Yes, Aunty Rose.' The little girl smiled trustingly at Rose.

It irritated him that Rose had somehow taken charge, but there wasn't much he could do right now. Not without creating a scene and upsetting Daisy at bedtime, which he wasn't willing to do. It wasn't his little niece's fault. And he should be protecting her, not putting yet more disorder into her life.

'Goodnight, Princess. Sleep well,' Leo said. He had to walk across the room and lean across Rose to kiss his niece goodnight. Bad move. Because Rose's perfume was the sexiest thing he'd smelled in weeks, and it was oh, so tempting to move back very slightly and kiss her, too.

He yanked his self-control back in place, just in time, then left the room and headed for the kitchen. Which was absolutely spotless. Well, Rose had left the dinner things to air-dry on the draining-board, but apart from that everything was clean and tidy. Maybe he'd overreacted about the living room. He made himself a cup of coffee and sat at the kitchen table.

Everything about Rose Carter set his teeth on edge. From the boho chic of her dress, to her chaotic lifestyle, to the sweet vanilla scent of her perfume. Like a topnote for rich, dark chocolate. It made him want to taste her, when really he should want to throttle her. Rose really wasn't good for Sara. She'd encouraged Sara to drop out of college when Sara had fallen pregnant; and, worse, he knew Rose had been in court charged with handling stolen goods. He'd hoped that maybe Sara would grow out of the friendship—he'd already learned the hard way that Sara did the opposite of whatever her family suggested, so he hadn't made a big issue of it—but it seemed that Rose was still hanging round his sister and dragging her down.

There were pictures pinned to the corkboard on the wall next to the kitchen table. Pictures of Daisy and Sara dressed in the same kind of boho chic as Rose. Second-hand clothes. In one picture, Sara and Rose had their arms draped round each other, giggling—the best of friends. Like sisters.

But Sara didn't need a substitute sister. She had three older brothers—brothers who adored her and spoiled her stupid as the baby of the family. Brothers who'd always looked after her. Though Joe and Milo were both working in Brussels for the next six months so Leo, as the eldest, had the sole responsibility for looking out for Sara. And he was doing his best, trying to juggle a crazy schedule at work with keeping an eye on his sister and making sure she didn't get into an even bigger mess—because Sara just attracted chaos.

And one of the biggest bits of chaos was in the shape of Rose Carter.

Then Rose walked in and closed the kitchen door behind her. It felt as if all the air had been sucked out of the room and the temperature had just gone up ten degrees. Ha. Leo wasn't scared of her. At a little over six feet tall, he was a good seven or eight inches taller than she was. She'd shed the tiara and the boa, but was still barefoot. And slender. He could easily pick her up, dump her outside the flat and lock the door, if he chose.

Though thinking about lifting her up wasn't a good idea. Because it made him think about pinning her against the wall and kissing the pulse that throbbed at the base of her neck. Before having wild, wild sex.

And he had the nasty feeling that she knew it.

'So,' she said, very quietly. 'You've decided to honour your sister with a visit. Shame she's not here.'

Honour Sara with a visit? That rankled—Rose made it sound as if he never bothered with his sister. Which was very, very far from the case. 'Not that it's any of your business, I ring her three times a week,' he said stiffly.

Rose shrugged. 'If you say so.'

Was she suggesting that he was lying? Leo felt his jaw tense. Of *course* he rang Sara three times a week! He'd even set an alarm on his laptop, so if he was working on a pile of case notes he wouldn't get so sidetracked by his work that he'd forget to call her. And he took Daisy out one Saturday a month. He'd ring and visit more often except he knew his little sister would complain he was smothering her or checking up on her and cramping her style. He'd thought he was managing a very tricky tightrope rather well.

But clearly Sara thought otherwise and was claiming he didn't bother with her. Which annoyed him even more. He'd given up on his sister for about a month, just after she'd dropped out of college—simply because he'd been fed up with sorting out her mistakes, he'd realised that she never took any notice of the advice he gave her, and he'd thought that maybe letting her stand on her own two feet for a change might give her a different perspective and make her grow up a bit. It hadn't, so he'd gone back to keeping an eye on her. But Sara had never quite forgiven him for taking that big step back.

He could explain this to Rose…though he didn't see what business it was of hers. Or why her opinion of him should matter. So instead he folded his arms and retreated into silence.

'Thank you for making me a coffee, by the way,' Rose added.

The sarcasm stung—the more so because she'd made him sound thoughtless, selfish and rude. 'Sarcasm is the lowest form of wit. And I didn't know how long you'd be. There was no point in letting a cup of coffee go cold.'

'No.' She walked over to the kettle and switched it on. Even though her dress was ankle-length and perfectly demure, Leo was still aware of how good her legs were and the faint swish of her dress made him think of the sound the material would make as it pooled at her feet—just before he lifted her and those beautiful legs wrapped round his waist and his body eased into hers.

Ah, hell. He argued niceties as a living. He was good at it. But Rose Carter made him tongue-tied. His libido simply took over his brain and supplied enough images to make him wary of speaking, in case he said any of his thoughts aloud. It was one of the reasons he never actually said her name—he was scared it might come out as a hiss of pure desire.

How was it possible to detest someone yet want them so badly at the same time?

'Want a refill?'

And she'd managed to wrong-foot him again. Just when he was working himself up for a fight with her, she turned on the courtesy. Did everything he hadn't done.

'No. Thanks,' he added belatedly.

'Suit yourself.' Just to rub it in, she didn't make herself a coffee. She used some kind of teabag—something that turned the water a dark ruby colour. He wasn't going to ask. Even though it smelled enticing—sweet, fruity, spicy, something he couldn't quite place—he wasn't going to ask.

She came to sit at the table opposite him. 'So what's the problem?'

You are.

Sitting this close, he could smell her perfume as well as the fruit tea. Soft and sexy and bewitching. All he had to do was reach out and he could touch her. Find out if her skin was as soft as it looked. Find out just how silky those corkscrew curls were. Find out just how well her lips would fit against his own.

He pulled himself together. This wasn't about Rose. It was about Sara and Daisy. Sara was old enough to look after herself; Daisy wasn't. 'It's time Sara started facing her responsibilities.'

Rose scoffed. 'She does.'

'Oh, really?' Leo spread his hands in exasperation. 'Let me see. She kicks up hell to go to art college—then, just as my parents had accepted that maybe she had made the right choice for her instead of acting on a whim, she drops out. So they were right all along. She would never have stuck it out.'

Rose folded her arms. 'Listen to yourself! What was she supposed to do—try and cope with settling in to motherhood and study at the same time? Come on. It was obvious she needed to take a year out.'

'But she's never gone back, and Daisy's almost five. She doesn't have a proper job or even a routine; she just muddles through doing this and that. And then she disappears for the weekend on a whim and dumps Daisy on just about anyone who's available.'

The smug, insufferable, conceited…Rose counted to ten. And then did it all over again so she'd manage to keep her voice calm and even when she spoke. 'Maybe you should try supporting her, for a change.'

'Like you do?' His voice was as soft as hers but held just as much of an edge. 'Mmm, you've done a great job. You introduced her to Paris Randall in the first place, if I remember correctly.'

The art student who'd swept Sara off her feet, got her pregnant, then vanished when he realised that Sara's family wasn't going to keep them both in luxury for the rest of their days. Paris had been doing one of the same course options as Rose, and they'd been talking in a coffee shop after a lecture when Sara had bounced in. Rose had introduced them—but she hadn't expected them to fall in love. Or for Paris—Paris, with his winsome smile and melting chocolate-brown eyes and adorable curly hair—to turn out to be so spineless and leave Sara to deal with the baby by herself.

'As you said, sarcasm is the lowest form of wit. And don't you think I already feel bad enough about Paris?' Rose asked.

Leo shrugged, as if to say, I don't give a damn what you feel.

He was cold, hard lawyer material. Exactly what Rose had run from becoming, all those years ago. She didn't like what Leo Ballantyne stood for—which was the main reason why she avoided him as much as possible. Sara's other brothers and her parents were almost as bad—all full of shoulds and musts and bossing her about. Stuffy in the extreme: they couldn't see just how much fun Sara was. Everything had to be wrapped up in responsibilities. 'Spontaneous' wasn't a word in their vocabulary.

'And then, of course, there's the court case,' Leo added.

Trust *him* to bring that up. 'The verdict upheld my innocence.'

He spread his hands. 'We both know that guilty people go to court and get off on a technicality.'

No smoke without fire. Mud stuck. Whatever cliché you used, it came down to the same thing. Rose's reputation had been sullied. She'd nearly lost her curator's job over it—and only the fact that she worked hard and was good at what she did had saved her. As it was, she had little hope of getting the job of her dreams. Because that damned court case was going to haunt her for years. The history of fashion was a small world—and, even though she was innocent, some people would still doubt her. People like Leo. People who played things by the book instead of trusting to their instincts. 'I wasn't guilty in the first place,' she said quietly. 'And I don't give a damn what you think of me.' Not quite true, but she wasn't going to go there right now. She lifted her chin. 'I know the truth, and that's what matters.' Even though the truth behind that was even more shameful.

He gave her a scathing look as if to say, You wouldn't know what the truth was if it jumped up and gave you a kiss.

And she couldn't meet his eyes. Not after thinking that word. *Kiss*. What would Leo's mouth be like when it was warm and soft with passion, instead of cold and hard with lawyerly cynicism? She'd never seen him smile. But if he was anything like his sister, that smile would light him up from the inside. He'd be absolutely stunning.

He coughed, and she realised he'd been speaking. She'd missed whatever he said. Lost in a flight of fancy about kissing Leo Ballantyne. Ha. Hell would freeze over before that ever happened. 'I'm sorry. You were saying?'

'My mother said she'd had a text from Sara. That she's gone off somewhere for the weekend.'

The way Leo said it, it sounded as if Sara had just dropped her responsibilities without a second thought and was gadding about somewhere. Rose had planned to be civil to him, but his attitude made her good intentions melt. 'You really are a narrow-minded bigot, aren't you? For your information, she's gone to a spa for the weekend. And before you start complaining about how much it costs to go to a spa and she's frittering away her money, it's an early birthday present. From me.'

'And what about Daisy?' Leo asked.

'I'm looking after her. Which was planned right from the moment I booked the spa. It was all part of the deal.' Rose resisted the urge to throw her tea over Leo. Just. 'Has it ever occurred to you what it's like, being a single mum? Day in, day out, you're the one who has all the responsibility. You're the one who makes all the choices. There's nobody there to take the weight off your shoulders, share the load. But Sara never complains. And I thought she deserved something special for her milestone birthday. Her twenty-fifth. A quarter of a century—worth celebrating, don't you think? A bit of me-time, a bit of spoiling, will do her good. But you lot are always so damned hard on her.'

'She can't just drop her responsibilities whenever she wants to,' Leo insisted. 'And she's got a family to support her.'

He called what they offered support? Rose shook her head. 'Do things your way or you'll harangue her until she does? If it wasn't for the physical resemblance, I'd say Sara was a changeling, because she's nothing like your family. She's worth more than the rest of you put together—and it's about time you lot understood that money isn't everything.'

His flinch told her the barb had hit home. Good. Rose already knew that Sara's family helped her financially. But that was only money. Sara was just the kid sister who'd gone off the rails and everyone was going to disapprove of her until she did what they told her to. Sara broke her heart over it—and Rose was the one who mopped up the tears.

'So what would you suggest we do, then?' Leo asked.

'Try putting yourself in her shoes—or at least see her for how she really is. Sara's a great mum. She works hard. And she's a damn good jewellery designer.' Sara had also enrolled in a part-time course to finish her degree—but she'd kept that from her family and Rose wasn't going to divulge any secrets. 'It wouldn't hurt you to come and play with Daisy once in a while. You might even find that she's a nice little girl who won't wipe mud all over your expensive Italian suit.' Rose had already registered the fabric and itched to touch it. She would have done, had it belonged to anyone else but Leo—but the disapproving look on his face made her wary of getting closer.

She suppressed the thought that the fabric wasn't the only thing she wanted to touch. The problem was, Leo Ballantyne was gorgeous. Tall, dark and beautiful: handsome really wasn't the right word to describe him. He was *beautiful*. His bone structure and colouring were stunning. She'd love to sketch him. To dress him. And then undress him. Slowly. Touch him until they were both quivering with need and desire—and their self-control would break at the same time…

But he was also the most formal, unreachable man she'd ever met in her life. He might be beautiful, but everything about him said 'don't touch.'

And it annoyed her enough to loosen her tongue. 'You know what's really sad about this? When I was a child, I remembered my uncles as the men who'd play silly games with me, who'd spin me round until I was dizzy, who'd tell me jokes, tickle me and take me to the zoo.'

He regarded her coolly. 'And you think I don't?'

'I know you don't,' Rose said hotly. 'Daisy sees you as the man who comes and tells her mummy off. And she doesn't even mention Joe and Milo.'

He recoiled slightly, then lifted his chin and gave her a cold, hard stare. 'They work in international law. They're not in the country very much.'

She already knew that—and he knew she knew it. 'And when they are, they don't make time for Sara. You all go on about how she's your "little sister"—but you see her as a possession, not a person. A possession who should act in the way you dictate. You've all decided her place in the family, and that's how you're always going to see her. If she doesn't fit, you'll punish her until she does.'

Leo's grey eyes narrowed. Cold and glittering. Like a newly sharpened sword. 'Just who are you to judge me?'

'Her best friend. The person who's *here*.'

'So you've moved in, now?'

Rose caught the implications and glared at him. He thought she was a freeloader as Paris had turned out to be? 'Don't be ridiculous. I have my own place. But I'm staying here for the weekend, yes. It's less upheaval for Daisy than taking her back to my flat.'

'That's not necessary,' Leo said. 'I'm her uncle. I'll look after her.'

Rose scoffed. 'You wouldn't have a clue where to start. You have no idea what her routine is, what she likes to eat, what she likes to play with.'

'Of course I do.'

'No. You just have this set idea of what children should be like—and what Sara should be like.'

'Sara's a walking magnet for chaos,' Leo said.

'She doesn't live in regimented order, I admit,' Rose said.

'You can't, if you have a child. But it'll only take me ten minutes to put Daisy's toys away—and then this flat will look spotless.'

'What about all that laundry everywhere?'

Rose rolled her eyes. 'That's not laundry. That's my work. Which I intend to do this evening, while Daisy's asleep.'

There was nothing he could say to that, she knew; and, just as she'd expected, he changed tack. 'It's not just the flat and the fact she's disorganised. She's hopeless with money. Worse, she's an easy target for con artists.'

True, Rose knew; she'd bailed her best friend out a few times. Though she really hoped Leo wasn't calling *her* a con artist. Because if he was, she might just be forced to kick him in the shins. 'She's getting better. But nagging her about it is only going to make her more stubborn. Moan at her for wasting money, and she'll go and fritter what she has, just for the hell of it. Whereas if you get her to work it out for herself—so she can see what her priorities are, where she'll be short if she goes on a frittering session, and where she'll have money to play with if she doesn't—she's fine. Try empowering her instead of treating her like a little kid who blows all her pocket money in the sweetshop.'

Leo shook his head in seeming disbelief. 'This is bizarre.'

'What?'

'I'm a lawyer. I'm used to summing people up swiftly—and I do it well. And here you are, lecturing me on psychology and the way you think I misread my sister?'

'You do misread her.'

'And you're an expert on people, are you?'

Rose shrugged. 'I'm a market stall trader. I meet people from all walks of life.' Not to mention the therapy she'd had when she was twenty. 'So, yes, I'd say I know a fair bit about people.' She folded her arms. 'And I'm not leaving Daisy with you. Sara entrusted her to me.'

'I'm Sara's oldest brother. Daisy will be perfectly safe with me.'

'Safe, yes. Happy—I doubt it.'

'And how do I know she's going to be safe with you?' he countered.

'She will be.' Rose stared coolly at Leo. 'I'm not making a

small child miserable just because you have a bee in your bonnet. A misguided one, too. You don't like me. Fine. I can live with that. But you also don't know me. Without all the facts, you're not in a position to make a valid judgement.'

'Anyone would think that you were a lawyer.' Leo stared at her with barely concealed dislike.

I nearly was, Rose thought. And it nearly finished me off. 'I don't think there's anything more to say. And I'm sure you have things to do—I certainly do. So perhaps you'd like to use your door key. On the way out.'

'You're throwing me out?'

'No. I'm suggesting that we have nothing left to discuss. And as neither of us would choose to spend time with the other socially, I'm sure you can think of a more productive—more *profitable*—use of your time.'

'This isn't over,' Leo warned.

She couldn't resist it. She spread her hands. 'So sue me,' she drawled.

Leo's lip curled, but he said nothing. He simply left. Not a slammed door, not a bold gesture. He just left. Rose heard the front door click behind him. And that was that.

Thirty seconds later, she'd double-locked the door and put the chain across it. She checked on Daisy—who was fast asleep, clutching her teddy with one arm—then tidied the toys away and set out her sewing box. She had hems to repair and buttons to match. And she wasn't going to think about Leo Ballantyne and his beautiful mouth. Not once.

CHAPTER TWO

LEO knew he shouldn't have walked out. But, he reasoned, Daisy was asleep in bed, and Rose clearly had the little girl's welfare at heart so she wouldn't do anything stupid such as go out and leave Daisy on her own. His niece would be safe until the morning. He could go back first thing and make sure that Rose was going to look after Daisy properly during the day—and the easiest way was to oversee it himself. Even if it meant he had to spend time with Rose.

By the time he got back to his own flat, he'd had time to think about everything Rose had said. It was the longest conversation he could ever remember having with her. And it galled him that she seemed to think he was a control freak who'd never bothered getting to know his niece. Did Daisy really think he was an ogre who did nothing but tell her mummy off? Yet the little girl was always pleased to see him on their special Saturdays out. It didn't add up.

Maybe Sara had been the one to say it to Rose, not Daisy. Maybe Daisy didn't talk about him to Rose. Daisy hadn't actually said that much to Leo about Rose, either, other than that she had pretty dresses and always smelled nice. He'd never managed to find out just how much influence Rose had over his niece.

Rose Carter was flaky and unreliable. A second-hand clothes dealer who'd been in trouble with the law. But what she'd yelled at him in temper… Hmm. It sounded as if she looked out for Sara and even had a strategy about keeping Sara on the rails financially. So, instead of being an even wilder child than Sara, Rose might have grown up. Might be a steadying influence, even.

Might being the operative word.

There was the stolen goods issue…but maybe Rose really had been innocent and hadn't just got off on a technicality. Maybe he'd been unfair to her. Doubly so, because he'd been fighting his attraction to her and had used any excuse to dislike her. He didn't want to be attracted to a bad girl—especially as he didn't have time for a social life right now. To get the promotion he wanted, he really had to put the hours in. He couldn't afford to let anything—anyone—distract him.

So why couldn't he get Rose Carter out of his head?

Leo still didn't have an answer for that one, the following morning. Though when he arrived at Sara's flat and there was no answer to his ring—and all the curtains appeared to be drawn back—he used the key to let himself into the flat. Called Daisy's name. Called Rose's.

No answer.

The flat was tidy—but empty. A tight ball of panic formed in his stomach. Where were they? Had Rose done some kind of moonlight flit with his niece? He had no idea what Rose's mobile phone number was, and, despite a quick look in the most obvious places, he couldn't see Sara's address book. Last night, Rose hadn't said anything about going out somewhere with Daisy today. He'd expected her to be the sort to lie in bed until midday and she'd barely be awake when he called this morning.

Clearly he'd got it wrong.

So where the hell was she?

Then it clicked. Rose was a market trader. Which meant that she had a stall. And the chances were, she was there—even though she was supposed to be looking after Daisy. Weekends were the busiest times at Camden market; thousands of tourists descended on the place in search of a bargain. OK, there were several sites to choose from—the Stables, Camden Lock, the Canal and Buck Street—but he had a feeling that everyone would know Rose Carter. All he had to do was ask…

* * *

'Sex-god alert.' Janey moved from the back of her stall to Rose's and dug her elbow into Rose's ribs. 'Look over there.'

Rose smiled to herself. It was Janey's mission in life to get Rose interested in a man. She said it would be good for Rose to go out with someone and get over what had happened with Steve. Rose thought otherwise. Her judgement of men was absolutely lousy—Steve had proved that once and for all—and no way was she risking getting hurt again. She was staying quite happily single, thank you very much. She had a job she loved, good friends, a family who loved her back and a god-daughter she adored. She didn't need anything else. And she definitely didn't need the complication of a love life.

'Oh, man. If I had a bucket of water, I'd throw it over him—can you just imagine if that T-shirt was wet? Oh, those muscles.' Janey fanned herself. 'He is *built*. I definitely wouldn't kick that out of bed.'

Rose laughed. 'It sounds like you're the one who needs the cold water, Janey!'

Then her smile faded as she saw where Janey was pointing.

Every female eye in the place was drawn to him—and with good reason. Even though the market was crowded, Leo Ballantyne stood out from the bargain-hunters and tourists. He was wearing faded jeans—snug enough to show off his extremely attractive gluteal muscles—a plain white T-shirt and a pair of dark glasses. Quite ordinary clothes, but a far from ordinary man.

Rose had never seen Leo in casual clothes before. In a dark suit, sober tie and white shirt, he was gorgeous but remote. In casual clothes, he was something else.

Touchable.

And it was all too easy to imagine peeling those jeans off him, sliding her hands under his T-shirt to touch his bare skin. Discovering its texture and temperature for herself. Then growing bolder, exploring with her lips...

Uh. Someone had squeezed glue into her mouth. That was the only reason why her tongue was stuck to the roof of her mouth and she couldn't breathe.

'Told you,' Janey said, laughing. 'Even you couldn't say no to that!'

Then it was Janey's turn to go silent as Leo reached Rose's stall. And smiled. A full-wattage, proper smile. A smile that made Rose's knees so weak that she had to grab the edge of her stall for support.

'Hello, Rose.'

This wasn't happening. She had to be dreaming. Leo never used her name—it was a point with him. If he didn't acknowledge her name, he could continue to regard her as beneath his notice. And he definitely never smiled at her. She'd have remembered a smile like that. The kind of smile that lit up the whole world.

She folded her arms and surreptitiously pinched the skin in the crook of her elbow. 'Ow.'

So she wasn't dreaming.

'Are you OK?' he asked, sounding genuinely concerned.

'Uh—yes.' No way was she going to admit to Leo Ballantyne what she'd just done. It would be way too embarrassing.

He pushed his dark glasses back over his hair. 'Where's Daisy?'

Oh, so *that* was what this was all about. She sighed and indicated the area at the back of her stall. 'Here. Drawing me some very pretty pictures.'

'Have you come to tell Aunty Rose off?' Daisy asked, peering up from her seat behind Rose.

Leo smiled at her. 'No. Lawyers don't just tell people off, you know.'

'Lawyer?' Although Janey had moved back to her own stall, she'd clearly been listening to the conversation. She returned to stand next to Rose and drew herself up to her full five feet one inch, folding her arms across her extremely ample bosom and jutting her chin at him. 'If you've come to hassle her, you're in the wrong place. Rose Carter is totally straight. Everyone knows she's completely above board.'

'I'm not here in an official capacity.' Leo smiled at her and held out his hand. 'Leo Ballantyne. Pleased to meet you.'

'Ballantyne? As in...?' Janey looked at Daisy, then back at Leo.

Leo nodded. 'Sara's brother. Daisy's uncle.'

'Hmm,' Janey said, pointedly not taking his hand. 'I'll be right next door if you need me, Rose.'

'Thanks,' Rose said.

Leo raised an eyebrow. 'What was that about?'

How did she explain this? 'Long story,' she prevaricated. Leo wouldn't take kindly to the fact that his sister talked about him and the rest of his family in less than glowing terms—and as a result most of the traders around Rose's patch in Camden were less than enthusiastic about the Ballantyne tribe.

'I haven't come to fight.'

No?

Her doubt must have been written all over her face, because he sighed. 'Look, I admit I wanted to check up on you. Make sure that Daisy was all right. But I haven't come to have an all-out fight with you.' He took a deep breath. 'I thought about what you said last night. And maybe we've got off on the wrong foot.'

Was she hearing things? Leo was actually admitting he was in the wrong?

'Rose?'

She was having trouble getting her head round this one. 'Did you just admit you were wrong about me?'

He had the grace to blush. Just a little bit. And, Lord, it made him attractive. That slight air of vulnerability. Only for a moment: but it showed there was another man behind the hard lawyer's façade. A softer, gentler man who actually felt things.

'Though it goes both ways,' he added. 'For your information, I ring Sara three times a week and I take Daisy out one Saturday a month. I'd do it more often, except Sara would say I was being a control freak and taking over her parental responsibilities.'

'First I've heard of it,' Rose said, lifting her chin.

'Sara overdoes the bit about being the poor little rich girl whose family just doesn't understand her.' Leo lifted a shoulder. 'Ask Daisy if you don't believe me.'

'She says you tell Sara off.'

He shrugged again. 'I probably do. It's habit. She's my baby sister and I'm used to sorting things out for her when she gets into a muddle. Which is quite often.'

Rose didn't know what to say.

'It's how she is,' Leo said quietly. 'I love my baby sister to bits, but I see her for who she is, too. She's a drama queen and a chaos magnet. It used to drive me crazy. Now I accept that and we don't fight so much.'

Something was wrong here. The Ballantynes all frowned on Sara and her lifestyle. Rose had even heard the occasional message on Sara's answering machine—Leo sounding exasperated and disapproving. But here he was, saying that Sara exaggerated...

Though Rose knew he was right. Sara was fun to be with, but she *was* a bit of a drama queen. And a chaos magnet. Leo had summed her up accurately.

And he'd said he loved his baby sister to bits.

And he took Daisy out.

So did this mean that all these years she'd got *him* wrong, too? That she'd failed to see through Sara's dramatic prose and missed how her family really felt about her? That Sara's family actually loved her as much as Rose's own family loved and supported her?

For once, Rose found herself lost for words.

'I didn't realise you were working today,' Leo said.

And his voice was carefully neutral. He didn't sound as if he was about to let her have it with both barrels. OK. She'd tell him the truth. 'I wasn't intending to. Except the friend who was going to run the stall for me went down with food poisoning in the middle of the night. I couldn't get anyone else to step in at such short notice.'

'I see.'

Not with that carefully schooled expression, he didn't. And she didn't want him to go back to being the disapproving, stuffy barrister she'd first encountered. She wanted that smile back. That gorgeous, full-wattage smile. All for her. 'This is peak business time for me, Leo. I have to pay my site fees whether I'm here or not.' And her budget was very finely balanced. Thanks to Steve, she couldn't afford not to be here. She still had debts to pay off. Debts that should never have been hers. 'It's not ideal,

I know, but Daisy'll be fine. She's got a stock of paper and pens, and Janey next door'll mind my stall for a couple of minutes whenever I need to take Daisy to the loo or get her something to eat or drink. I have no intention of neglecting her. She's my best friend's daughter—and my god-daughter. Which makes her practically family.'

He didn't correct her there, she noticed. She'd expected him to argue legal niceties, such as the fact she wasn't actually related to Daisy. Instead, he looked thoughtful. 'There is another way.'

'You'll run my stall for me?' She snorted. 'Hardly.'

'You don't think I can?'

'Unless you've always been interested in vintage clothes—which, somehow, I doubt—then no. You don't know my stock. And I doubt you know how to haggle.'

'I haggle for a living,' he pointed out.

As a barrister, yes. 'Court isn't quite the same as the market.'

His expression said that he was dying to prove her wrong and accept the challenge. But then he smiled again, and it was enough to turn Rose's knees decidedly wobbly. 'I'll concede that. And that I don't know much about vintage clothes. No, what I meant was, I can look after Daisy today.'

Her eyes narrowed. 'I don't think so.'

'You said yourself this wasn't ideal. And, as I told you, I take Daisy out once a month. So why don't I spend today with her—sneak in an extra day together? If it makes you feel better, I could do whatever you were planning to do with her.'

Last night, he'd said he didn't think she was responsible enough to look after his niece. Attacking hadn't worked. So was this a backdoor way of getting Daisy away from her? Charm the child away?

She folded her arms and shook her head. 'Sara left her in my care.'

He sighed. 'Look, Rose, I know we have our differences. But we both have Daisy's best interests at heart. It's not as if you don't know who I am. And I'm hardly going to abduct my own niece.'

Rose wasn't so sure. 'She'll be fine with me. She knows the market, and everyone around here knows her.'

'She's here with you a lot?'

That sounded like a trick question. Something he could use to prove that Sara neglected her little girl. Leo's trade was in words—and, from bitter experience, Rose knew that barristers would twist your words to suit them. So she had to be very, very careful what she said. 'Sara used to spend time around here when Daisy was very small,' Rose explained. 'She's safe here. This is a community where people look out for each other.'

Leo shoved his hands into his pockets, as if trying to hide his irritation. 'What time do you finish?'

'Five. Though I'll probably start packing up at four.'

'OK. Let me put it another way. Daisy's four years old. She's not going to want to sit here drawing all day. She needs to run around and burn off some energy.'

This was surreal. She'd thought Leo was the type who thought children should be seen and not heard. Who disapproved of kids running around or making noise.

Had she got it so wrong?

'Why don't I take her out for the day while you're working? I'll leave you my mobile-phone number—and if you give me yours, I can text you to let you know where we are or ring you if I hit a snag. And I'll meet you back at Sara's place at six o'clock,' he finished.

It all sounded reasonable. Way too reasonable for a man like Leo Ballantyne. 'I'll check it with Sara,' Rose said, pulling her mobile phone from the moneybelt she wore loosely round her hips.

'Fine. But I thought you said this was a weekend to recharge Sara's batteries? She'll worry something's wrong if you ring her, and she won't relax.'

True. Which was why Rose hadn't mentioned Leo's visit when Sara had called this morning—and luckily Daisy had still been asleep, so the little girl hadn't told her mum either.

'Let her enjoy her spa. I promise you, Daisy won't come to any harm in my care.'

Rose shook her head. 'This isn't…You never admit you're wrong. Or to any weakness. You're a Ballantyne.'

'Actually, I always admit when I'm wrong. It just doesn't

happen very often. I think this might even be a first.' His mouth quirked. 'And I take back everything I said about you not being responsible. You're more suspicious than I am. Do you want me to leave you some surety—my car keys or my house keys—to make sure I don't run off with Daisy and hold her to ransom until Sara agrees to go back and live with my parents or something?'

For a moment, Rose was tempted to say yes.

The quirk turned into a proper smile. 'You really think I'd do that?'

'I don't know,' Rose said honestly.

Leo spread his hands. 'Think about it. I'm a barrister. If I kidnap my niece and you go to the press, what's that going to do to my career?'

Wreck it. Just as the press had pretty much wrecked hers. Of course he wouldn't take a risk like that. She sighed. 'OK. I'll trust you. As long as Daisy's happy to go with you, that is. But you check in with me every hour, on the hour. And I want to speak to my god-daughter when you call, so I'm absolutely sure she's all right.'

'Agreed. And I'll call you if I have any problems that can't be solved by something pink and sparkly or a story.' Leo took his mobile phone from his jeans pocket, switched it on and handed it to her. 'Take my number yourself so you're sure you have the right one. And perhaps you'd programme yours into my phone for me?'

It was the first time her fingers had ever touched his. And she really wasn't prepared for the sheer surge of energy. How could one small touch make her feel as if she were sitting on top of an active volcano?

She dragged in a breath and put her number into his phone. Under R. CARTER, to make it look professional. Which it was: they were only in contact because of Daisy. There was nothing else personal between them. She flicked into another screen to pick up his number, and added it to her phone.

'Thank you,' he said quietly when she handed the phone back to him.

'Daisy, would you like to go out with Uncle Leo for the day?' Rose asked.

The little girl looked up from her drawing and her eyes widened. 'Like our special Saturdays?'

Uh-oh. So Leo had been telling the truth. Why had Sara kept it quiet? The way she'd always spoken about her family... could it be that she'd added a lot more colour to make a good story out of it? That the Ballantynes weren't all stuffy and repressed and sticklers for how things should be done?

'Aunty Rose has to be here on the stall today,' Leo said. 'Maybe you and I can go where Aunty Rose said she'd take you today?'

'The 'Quarium, to see the sharks?' Daisy asked.

He gave her an indulgent glance. 'What, again? But, yes, if that's what you want, sweetheart. We'll go and see the sharks.'

'And we can have ice cream?'

'Only if you eat your lunch.'

Rose and Leo both said it at the same time, then stared at each other. She could see quite clearly on his face that he hadn't expected her to be as strict as he was on that point. And in turn she was surprised that he'd thought to put in a condition instead of playing the favourite uncle who'd say yes to everything and to hell with Sara's rules.

'And we can have spaghetti for lunch?' Daisy asked.

'That's proper spaghetti, not the tinned stuff,' Rose added swiftly.

Leo looked amused. 'I know that. We can have spaghetti, Daisy—that little Italian place you like in Covent Garden.'

'The one where they give me a special lolly?' She whooped. 'Can I go, please, Aunty Rose?'

Rose ruffled her hair. 'Remember the rules?'

'Stay close to Uncle Leo and do what he tells me when we're out,' Daisy said promptly. 'I always do.'

'And what do you do if you get separated on the tube?' Rose asked.

'Find a guard and tell him Uncle Leo's name,' Daisy recited.

'Attagirl.' Rose hugged her god-daughter. 'You have a lovely day.' She looked at Leo and dropped her voice. 'And I expect a call from you every hour, on the hour.'

'You'll get it,' Leo said. 'And, Rose?'

'Yes?'

'You're right. I don't haggle as well as you do.' For a moment, he stared at her mouth. 'Maybe that's something I should work on.'

Was Leo flirting with her, now? Rose was sure she was hyperventilating. Because that look and those words had put a completely different image into her brain. An image of Leo's mouth working on hers. Of those beautiful lips teasing hers. Coaxing her into opening her mouth and letting him deepen the kiss. Of his tongue flicking against hers, mimicking the motion of a deeper intimacy.

She didn't trust herself to speak. Just watched Leo walking away, hand in hand with Daisy. And she prayed she was doing the right thing.

CHAPTER THREE

THE first call was late, and Rose was about to yell at Leo when he said, 'We were delayed on the tube. I couldn't get a signal.'

'Oh.' The breath—and the fight—hissed out of her.

'We're outside the Aquarium. I'll put Daisy on.'

Two seconds later, Daisy was jabbering excitedly into the phone. 'We're going to see the sharks. And we might go on a boat down the river, 'cos it's sunny. And we're going to have spaghetti. And Uncle Leo thinks my jokes are *really* funny.'

Rose chuckled. Daisy knew three jokes, and she always got the punchline wrong. And she liked to tell them over and over again. 'I'm glad you're having a nice time.'

'Uncle Leo's nice,' Daisy confided. 'He's got a lovely smile. What's sex on legs?'

Rose choked. 'Why?'

''Cos I heard a lady say that's what Uncle Leo was.'

Priceless. Rose would have loved to see Leo's face right now.

Then her smile faded. Because that was a pretty good description of Leo Ballantyne. When he wasn't being disapproving, he was delicious. 'So what is it, then?' Daisy asked, clearly impatient when Rose didn't answer immediately.

'Ask Uncle Leo. Have a nice time, sweetheart. Speak to you soon.'

But before she could hang up, Leo was on the phone again. 'I'll call you in an hour. But if I can't get a signal, then I'll call you as soon as I can. It doesn't mean I've absconded.'

Rose could hear Daisy piping up in the background. 'What's ab—ab—?'

'You'll find her favourite word is "why,"' Rose said.

'Of course. She's a barrister's niece.' Leo sounded amused rather than appalled. 'And she never stops talking.'

'She's only four. Don't suppress her.'

The amusement in his voice faded abruptly. 'We'll have this conversation later.'

Uh-oh. That didn't bode well.

Rose did her best to concentrate on her stall. Talking to customers about vintage clothes, discussing colours and textures and cut—usually it was something that absorbed her. But today she kept thinking of Leo. Of just how good he'd looked in those jeans. Of that smile, the unexpected warmth in his eyes.

And he'd admitted he'd been wrong.

She couldn't remember the last time a man had done that. Steve certainly hadn't.

Though Leo was nothing like Steve.

Leo was like nobody she'd ever met.

And she pushed the thought away: it was way, way too scary.

The second call was two hours later. 'We had to go back and see the sharks four times. But I've taken photographs with my phone, to prove we were there.'

'I trust you,' she said. Considering their history, they were the last words she should have said. But she meant it. Leo Ballantyne had his faults—but he also had integrity.

'So do I still have to call in on the hour?'

'Yes.' Because when he wasn't being disapproving, he had a gorgeous voice. Cultured. Slightly posh. Dead sexy. And she rather liked hearing it.

'We're going for spaghetti and ice cream now.'

'Don't let her have fizzy drinks,' Rose said promptly. 'And don't let her con you. Fizzy water mixed with orange juice—and I mean juice, not squash—is fine. The sugary stuff, absolutely not.'

'My sentiments exactly.' There was a hint of amusement in his voice again. 'I thought I was meant to be the stern, disapproving one? I think you could give me a run for my money, Rose Carter.'

'Yeah. I could.'

'Hmm. We're still having that conversation later.' Again, he passed her over to Daisy, who was bubbling over with facts and figures about sharks and fish.

'See you later, sweetheart,' Rose said. 'Enjoy your day.' Though, much as it irked her to admit it, she had a feeling that Daisy was going to enjoy herself a lot more with her Uncle Leo than she would have done sitting behind Rose's market stall. Even if Rose had let her make bracelets and play with beads all afternoon.

But what had really surprised her was the idea that Leo Ballantyne could be fun. Sara had always said he was boring and stuffy and never stopped nagging. From the little Rose had seen of him, she knew how good he was at disapproving. He'd always sounded exasperated and faintly weary whenever she'd heard him speak to Sara. As if his kid sister was a nuisance.

But that hint of amusement in his voice just now, the fact he hadn't minded listening to Daisy's jokes over and over again…maybe she'd misjudged him.

Or maybe not. Where men were concerned, she knew her judgement was lousy. And Leo Ballantyne definitely had control-freak tendencies. Not her type. At all.

Leo's third call was more plaintive. 'We're in a toy shop.' And he sounded out of his depth.

'Bad move,' Rose said. 'Let me guess. She's got you to buy her something pink and sparkly?'

'Fairy wings and a crown. With flashing lights.'

'Which she won't take off even to go to bed tonight,' Rose said.

'Doesn't matter. We can take them off when she's asleep.'

Without doubt the indulgent uncle. And Rose suppressed her emotions at the idea of them looking after a child together. She and Leo were not together and never would be. Plus she didn't see why he had to hang around when she'd finished work. She was perfectly capable of looking after Daisy. Why was he checking up on her?

'Are you vegetarian?' he asked.

'Why?'

'Because I'm cooking dinner.'

Rose pinched her inner arm again. It hurt—so she wasn't dreaming. Maybe she'd misheard. 'You're cooking dinner?'

'Don't sound so surprised. I'm perfectly capable of cooking.'

It wasn't *that* that had surprised her. He was a Ballantyne—practically perfect in every way, in his world view. Of course he could cook. He'd do it well, too. 'I wasn't expecting you to cook for me.'

'I'm cooking for Daisy and me. Might as well cook for three as for two. So are you?'

'Not quite. I eat fish.'

'OK. Here's Daisy.'

When Rose parked her battered estate car outside Sara's flat, she really wasn't sure what to expect. Would Leo be home already? He hadn't called her since the toy shop. Had he lulled her into a false sense of security with that offer of cooking dinner, and right now he'd taken Daisy to some safe house or other? Dread began to crawl up her spine. Please, no. Please don't let her have been taken for a fool again. There was too much at stake. Something much, much more valuable than just her reputation and her bank account and her flat and her career.

But when she unlocked the front door, she could smell lemon and ginger. Leo was sprawled on the floor in the living room, drawing pictures with his niece—who, as she'd expected, was wearing a crown and fairy wings. He looked up and smiled, and Rose's heart nearly stopped.

No. There were a lot of things wrong with this picture. Leo was not her husband, caring for their child while he waited for his wife to come home from work. That was not a look that said he'd greet her properly later—in private. Daisy was Rose's goddaughter, not her own child. And Rose didn't want to get married anyway. Not ever. Not after Steve.

'Hi. How was your day?' he asked.

Surreal. He even sounded like a loving husband. 'Fine, thanks.' Lie. She'd been on pins all day, worrying that she'd done the wrong thing. When you weren't used to small children, they could be overwhelming; and she also didn't want Daisy seeing the disapproving side of Leo. 'You?'

Daisy leapt up and ran towards Rose with her arms out. Rose scooped her into her arms and hugged her. 'The 'Quarium was really cool and the shark was huge. And look at my wings! They're really sparkly. Look, Aunty Rose, they flash.' She demonstrated the flashing lights on her fairy wings and chattered on happily; Rose just held her tightly, breathing in the strawberry scent of Daisy's hair. Thank God, this hadn't all gone pear-shaped.

'And I'm making you a picture,' Daisy finished. 'I drawed my name. A big duh for Daisy.'

'Dee,' Leo corrected.

'Duh,' Rose said firmly. 'They learn the alphabet by phonetic sound, nowadays.' Her gaze challenged him to argue with her; but he shrugged and backed down.

'And Uncle Leo got me a bead set,' Daisy added, wriggling in Rose's arms. 'It's all pink and glittery. I'm going to make bracelets for your stall, just like Mummy does.'

Leo looked interested. 'You sell Sara's jewellery?'

Rose sighed. 'Yes—and, before you ask, it's all completely above board. I have a book of her designs, so if people want to order a piece they can. And I've always had separate accounting for Sara's stock.' She set Daisy back on her feet. 'Want to show me your beads, sweetheart?'

Daisy nodded. 'I'm going to make Uncle Leo a bracelet, with a heart and a butterfly.'

Rose didn't dare look at Leo. 'I'm not sure he'd like a pink bracelet.'

''S all right, I'll do him a blue one 'cos he's a boy,' Daisy said solemnly.

'Ah, but he's a grown-up.' Rose couldn't resist the idea of winding Leo up thoroughly. No way would he ever wear a bracelet—he was way too conventional for that. Rose would head Daisy off at the last minute to make sure the little girl wasn't upset, but he deserved this. Deserved to see himself as he really was. Uptight and prissy. 'You could make him one from *my* beads, if you like.'

'Yay!' Daisy clapped her hands in delight.

Rose risked a glance at Leo; his face was expressionless. Then again, he was a barrister, used to playing things close to his chest.

'We'll do this while Uncle Leo's cooking,' Rose said, and grabbed her bead box.

'Don't you need to measure my wrist?' Leo asked as she cut a piece of elastic.

It would be a better fit if she did: but she wasn't quite sure she could cope with the idea of getting that close to him. 'No need. I can estimate.'

'OK. I know my place. I'll be in the kitchen if you need anything, Daisy,' he said, ruffling his niece's hair.

Meaning he didn't think she was capable of looking after Daisy herself? But he'd gone before she could make a smart response, and Daisy was clamouring to do threading. She decided to let it go—just this once, as to be fair she'd started it by offering to help Daisy make him a bracelet—and concentrated on the little girl.

Leo had expected Rose to be late. But she'd been pretty much on time. Any lateness could be down to traffic. She'd talked about having separate accounting for Sara's jewellery. Which was businesslike and efficient. And which didn't seem to gel with his idea of Sara's friends: the sort who made their decisions on the swing of a pendulum or the turn of a tarot card.

On the other hand, Rose had been accused of selling stolen goods. So maybe Sara had been the one to insist on proper accounting, to avoid any potential problems.

Ah, hell. What was it about Rose Carter that turned all his preconceptions back on themselves? Just when he thought he'd pigeon-holed her, she did something unexpected.

Once the potatoes were simmering nicely, Leo wandered back into the kitchen doorway and leaned against the jamb, watching Rose and his niece. Daisy had sorted beads into piles of different colours, and it seemed as if Rose was encouraging Daisy to count as she threaded the beads onto the elastic.

Hmm. Again, not what he'd expected. She was playing with the little girl but helping her learn at the same time. Making it fun. Loving and responsible at the same time.

When the bracelet was finished, Rose tied a knot in it for Daisy, then set out the tray of sparkly beads he'd bought earlier. Ones that had beads with letters on as well as the glittery ones: he'd been trying to sneak in the odd educational toy without Sara noticing.

To his surprise, Rose was getting Daisy to pick out the letters of her name.

'Duh for Daisy,' the little girl said, picking it out. 'A big duh.'

'They're all capitals. Can you remember what's next?'

'Ah for ant,' Daisy said. She looked thoughtfully. 'I can't see a ah.'

'I'll help you because this is a hard one.' Rose gave Daisy the capital A. 'What next?'

'Ih, like a little mouse squeaking ih ih ih,' Daisy said, promptly choosing an I. 'And then it's a suh. Like a snake, sss, sss, sss. Mummy's name starts with suh.'

'Well done,' Rose encouraged her. 'And the last one?'

'Yuh for yo-yo.' Daisy laid the last letter in place. 'That spells my name. Duh ah ih suh yuh. Daisy,' she said proudly.

'I didn't know she could read,' Leo said.

Rose glanced up, looking startled—clearly she'd been concentrating on Daisy and hadn't seen him in the doorway. 'She's four. She'll start school in September. And she's bright.'

'Course she is. She's a Ballantyne.'

'Uncle Leo, I did you your bracelet.' Daisy picked it up and danced over to him. 'You have to wear it.'

He glanced at Rose. Her expression told him she was expecting him to knock the child back, be dismissive. Ha. He wasn't *that* insensitive. Costume jewellery wasn't his style—at all—but he'd wear it for his niece. He smiled and held his right hand out. 'Do you want to put it on for me, Princess?'

'Oh, yes!' Beaming, Daisy slipped the sepia and black bracelet onto his hand. 'Look, it fits just right!'

Rose's estimate of his wrist size was spot on. Leo suppressed the tiny pang of regret that she hadn't actually touched him. He'd be civil to her until he was sure that she was going to look after Daisy properly. But he definitely didn't want to get involved. Even if Rose was turning out to be more sensible than he'd expected.

'It looks really pret—handsome,' Daisy corrected herself.

Leo grinned and ruffled her hair. 'Course it does. You made it for me.' He glanced at Rose. 'Dinner's in ten minutes.'

'Thank you,' she said quietly. 'I really didn't expect you to do that.'

He shrugged. 'As I said, I was cooking for two already. A third isn't much extra effort.' And it meant that he could keep an eye on Daisy. Make sure that Rose was going to look after her properly.

He squashed the thought that it was an excuse to get to see more of Rose.

Dinner was fabulous. Salmon baked in foil with lemon and ginger—Daisy's was plain, Rose noticed—with baby new potatoes, mange-tout and baby corn.

Daisy turned her nose up at the vegetables. Rose was about to step in and do some gentle nagging when Leo beat her to it.

'It's proper princess food,' Leo told his niece. 'The more you eat, the more your crown will sparkle.'

Daisy gave him a suspicious look. 'How do you know?'

Leo grinned. 'Because I know everything. Ask Mummy when she gets home.'

Rose squirmed. She'd heard Sara describe Leo as a know-all before now. Obviously he was well aware of that. Though there wasn't an edge to his voice.

Somehow, she felt wrong-footed. There was more to Leo than she'd thought. He was able to laugh at himself—which, if he was the stuffy, repressed man Sara always described him as, he wouldn't be able to do.

So if he wasn't just Sara's über-conventional big brother... that made him dangerous.

Because Rose was way too aware of how attractive he was. The way he'd drawn all eyes in the market this morning—including hers.

She suppressed a shiver. Nothing was going to happen between them. For a start, Daisy had to be her focus that weekend. And Leo didn't like her anyway. As soon as he realised that Rose was perfectly capable of looking after his niece, he'd leave her be. And she'd make very sure she avoided him in future.

'I, um—did you want to do Daisy's bath?' Rose asked, when dinner was finished. 'While I wash up, seeing as you cooked?'

Longing flickered briefly in his face. 'I've never done bathtime.'

This morning, Rose would've been sure that was because he'd never bothered. Now, she wondered if it was because Sara hadn't let him, trying to prove to Leo that she was perfectly capable of looking after her daughter all by herself.

Her mouth opened, to offer doing the bath together—and then closed abruptly. No. She'd be happier if they were in different rooms. Not too close. Especially after Janey's wet T-shirt comment. If Daisy splashed him and he stripped off that T-shirt...

Uh. She was way too young for hot flushes. Hoping he hadn't noticed the colour she felt rising in her cheeks, she said coolly, 'It's not difficult. I'm sure you can work it out. Just check the temperature of the water with your elbow before you let her get in.'

'Because children's skin is thinner and more sensitive than that of adults. I'm aware of that.' His gaze held hers for a moment. Telling her that he'd never, ever do anything to hurt Daisy. That he'd protect her at all costs.

For a second, Rose wondered what it would be like to have this man on your side. To know that he'd back you all the way, protect you. Then she shook herself. She didn't need protecting. She was doing fine on her own. 'Daisy will show you where the bubbles are,' she mumbled, and fled into the kitchen.

She'd just finished clearing up in the kitchen when she heard a pleasant tenor voice singing. Stopping every so often, as if to check something, then continuing. Daisy was clearly teaching Leo her favourite bath song, 'Five Little Ducks Went Swimming One Day.' And he was stopping to let her tell him how many ducks were left. Counting backwards from five. Teaching her and making it fun at the same time.

And, from the giggles she could hear, Rose could tell that
Daisy was enjoying herself thoroughly. Clearly she adored her
uncle. So why had Rose had no idea about this?

Leo's words echoed in her head. 'Sara overdoes the bit about
being the poor little rich girl whose family just doesn't understand
her.' He was absolutely right—and, worse, Rose had encouraged
Sara. She bit her lip. She'd misjudged Leo Ballantyne. Big time.
Daisy wasn't only safe with him, she was happy. Which meant
Rose definitely wasn't needed around here.

She didn't join Daisy and Leo in the bathroom. Instead, she
sat down with her accounts. Putting them in order would make
her concentrate, so she didn't have room to think. Room to feel
excluded and miserable.

She was most of the way through her accounts—and Sara's—
when Leo appeared in the living room. 'She'd like you to read
her a bedtime story. Apparently, boys can't do princess voices
properly. Would you mind?'

'Sure.' And then he could leave.

Except he didn't. When she'd settled Daisy and the little girl
was falling asleep, Rose returned to the living room to find Leo
sitting at the table on the chair next to hers, flicking through the
book of Sara's designs.

'She really is good at this.'

'Don't sound so surprised.'

He inclined his head in acknowledgement. 'I hadn't seen
these before.'

Why? Because he'd been so sure that Sara was slapdash about
her jewellery, he hadn't even bothered? Or—the nagging thought
crept into Rose's head—because Sara had refused to show him?

'The kettle's on. Would you like a coffee? Or one of those fruit
tea things?'

This was surreal. Why was Leo being so nice to her?

She realised she'd spoken aloud when he smiled. 'Maybe
we've misjudged each other. Sara keeps her life…' he paused,
as if searching for the right words '…somewhat compartmental-
ised,' he finished. 'And you look tired.'

'I'm fine, thanks. And I need to finish my books.'

'I didn't think you'd…well…'

Have any idea about business? Oh, she could see that. He obviously had her down as an airhead. 'Doing my accounts every day makes it a lot easier to keep on top of things, and saves a lot of time when I'm filling in the forms at the end of the tax year.' She folded her arms. 'Or are you mentally adding potential tax fraud to my list of crimes?'

He had the grace to wince. 'That wasn't what I meant. It's just that creative types don't often have a business head. My sister certainly doesn't.'

Oh. So he hadn't been sniping at her personally. 'I did Economics A level.'

He raised an eyebrow. 'Unusual choice for someone planning to do an art course.'

'I didn't apply to art college, first time round.' The words were out before she could stop them.

He said nothing, just waited. And she found herself explaining, 'The course I chose wasn't for me. I dropped out.' No way was she going to tell him she'd had a nervous breakdown over it. How unhappy she'd been, trying to make herself into somebody she wasn't and following a dream that wasn't hers. He already thought she was flaky. If he knew about her breakdown, he'd think she was unreliable as well. Or, worse, not suitable to be around Daisy. 'Luckily my family encouraged me to follow my dream, so I applied to art college. Where I met your sister.' Whereas the Ballantynes had been dead set against Sara going to art college, convinced that she wouldn't stick it out, that she'd get bored and change her mind halfway through the course. Sara had had to fight all the way for what she'd wanted. And Rose had supported her—just as Sara had supported Rose through a panic attack on her first day at art college. That was what friends did. Were there for each other.

'You wanted to be an artist?'

He sounded interested. So maybe it wouldn't hurt to tell him a little more. 'Not exactly. It was clothes I liked. I didn't want to design them myself, but I liked seeing how things changed over the years. I did some seminars on the history of costume, on restoration.' The bit she loved most, both in her museum work and on her market stall. Conserving old fabrics. Repairing them invisibly, so nobody would ever guess that there had once been moth holes or faded patches in a piece of silk.

He nodded. 'Ever thought about working in that area? Apart from your stall, I mean.'

She shrugged. 'There aren't that many costume museums—and full-time curator jobs aren't exactly thick on the ground.' The court case had made it a hell of a lot harder for her even to get an interview, let alone a job. Even though she hadn't been convicted, her world was small enough for everyone to know about the case. And mud—even when it actually belonged to someone else—stuck. For a long time. 'The stall means I can support myself. Anyway, I like what I do.' And she loved the community spirit among the market traders, the way they'd accepted her right from the start—the way they'd all been so firmly on her side, rooting for her and packing the spectator gallery in court to show their support. Helping her face the prosecutor with her head held high. 'I enjoy working with antique fabrics, mending vintage pieces invisibly and giving them a new lease of life.' She smiled. 'Daisy enjoys my button box, too. It's been great for teaching her colours and numbers.'

Rose Carter liked fixing things. And, from what she'd let slip earlier, Leo could see now it was one of the reasons she had become friendly with Sara. Because Sara—claiming that her family didn't understand her—would have seemed vulnerable, as if she needed fixing.

So maybe—just maybe—Rose wasn't quite what he'd always thought her to be.

Odd, though, that she wasn't really using her degree. If she had the skills and knowledge to be a curator, why was she working on a market stall? Why hadn't she set her ambitions any higher? Was she like his sister, at heart—someone who drifted from one day to the next and trusted tomorrow to look after itself? Or was something holding her back?

He finished his coffee. 'We need to talk about tomorrow.'

'Tomorrow?'

'Food poisoning takes a while to get over. So I assume your friend won't be up to manning your stall tomorrow.'

'Probably not. But Daisy and I will be fine.'

He realised that now. And he was really supposed to be working on some briefs. All the same… 'Why don't I spend the day with her again? We didn't manage to fit our river trip in. And I bet she'd love going round the gardens at Kew and spotting as many different pink flowers as she can.'

Rose's expression told him she was torn between letting Daisy have a nice day out, and wanting to look after Daisy herself—keeping her promise to Sara.

'Today worked out OK, didn't it?' he reminded her.

'Well—yes.'

'So tell me what time you're planning to leave tomorrow. I'll be here to pick up Daisy. And if you're feeling guilty about dumping her on me, she's my niece. I *like* spending time with her.'

'She's my responsibility,' Rose said.

Leo raised an eyebrow. 'Are you an only child?'

'No. I'm the youngest.' She frowned. 'What makes you say that?'

'Because you seem to have issues about sharing.'

Her eyes widened. 'I do not.'

'Then let me take Daisy on the river tomorrow. If Sara has a hissy fit about it when she gets back, that's not a problem.' He gave her a broad smile. 'I can out-hiss her. Not to mention pulling rank, as the oldest sibling.'

That grin did seriously strange things to her insides. And she really shouldn't let this happen. 'Do you always get your own way?' she fenced.

'Yes,' Leo said simply.

She wasn't sure whether that was a threat or a promise. There was no boasting, no arrogance in his tone: just assurance that he got his own way because he was right.

'So what time do you want me here tomorrow?' he continued.

She gave in to the inevitable. 'Quarter to nine?'

He nodded and headed for the door. 'Quarter to nine. I'll see you then.' And then that smile again as he paused and looked back at her. 'Don't forget to double-lock the door behind me.'

What did he think she was, a child who couldn't look after herself? No wonder he drove Sara crazy.

And yet that smile softened the comment. Maybe it wasn't a control thing. Maybe it was because he, like Rose, looked after people.

Maybe.

CHAPTER FOUR

AT PRECISELY quarter to nine the next morning, Leo arrived. Again, he was wearing casual clothes, this time faded jeans and a plain navy T-shirt. He hadn't shaved; although Rose normally found stubble a turn-off, on Leo it just emphasised his dark good looks. Made him look sexy as hell. Made her think of what he'd look like first thing in the morning, with slight shadows under his eyes. Shadows there because he hadn't had much sleep, because he'd been making love instead of sleeping.

Her libido wasn't just sitting up and begging, it was rolling over and demanding to have its tummy rubbed.

Stop it, she told herself. *He's here for Daisy. Not for you.*

'Hey, Princess.' He swept his niece up into the air and kissed her. 'Are you ready?'

Oh, yeah. I'm ready.

Rose squashed the thought. In her experience, good-looking men were trouble. Big trouble. She'd had enough hassles to last a lifetime. And Leo Ballantyne was the last man she'd get involved with. It would be just too complicated. His world wasn't a place where she wanted to be. She knew he despised her world; and, anyway, he was Sara's oldest brother. Sure, they could have a wild affair.

One hell of a wild affair.

But when it was all over, Rose's friendship with Sara could end up being part of the wreckage. And that would mean she wouldn't see Daisy any more, either. Something Rose wasn't prepared to risk.

Daisy giggled and hugged him. 'Aunty Rose said we're going 'sploring.'

'We're going to take a boat from Big Ben all the way down to Kew,' Leo told her. 'And we're going to see some very pretty flowers in a very special garden.'

'Will we see fairies?'

'We might do. We'll just have to look very carefully,' Leo said solemnly. He put his niece down again and looked at Rose.

Lord, his eyes were beautiful. A soft, sexy grey. She could imagine how they'd heat up in passion. Go darker. Then he'd smile. A slow, sensual smile that promised she'd be in a different universe for a while. Forgetting time. Forgetting everything but his hands and his mouth tracking over her body. Forgetting everything except the way he brought every nerve ending zinging to life.

'We'll see you later, then.'

His words cut into her daydream, and she could feel the colour rush into her cheeks. She just hoped he hadn't been able to read her thoughts. 'Sure,' she said coolly.

And she ignored the swoop of disappointment when he didn't kiss her goodbye.

Stupid, stupid, stupid. Of course he wasn't going to kiss her goodbye. She was nothing to him—just his kid sister's friend. One he didn't even like very much. Kissing, Leo Ballantyne and Rose Carter just didn't go together.

And she'd be extremely stupid even to think about it.

All the same, she couldn't shift the mood; even setting up her stall didn't take her mind off Leo. Or the sneaky, whining wish that he'd asked her to skip her stall for today and go with him and Daisy.

To hell with the money. If he'd asked her, she would've gone.

'You all right, Rose?' Janey asked.

'Sure,' Rose fibbed.

'That brother of Sara's wasn't giving you any hassle, was he?'

'No,' Rose said. Not intentionally, anyway. And she'd wrestle her libido back under control soon enough. All she had to do was think about Steve and the wreckage he'd left in her life. Her promise to herself that she'd never, ever lay herself open to something like that again. OK, so Leo wasn't Steve. But she knew that the emotional wreckage Leo would leave behind would be far more painful.

And she wasn't going to go there.

'Hmm,' Janey said, but to Rose's relief the conversation didn't get a chance to go any further when the first customers arrived.

Leo, sitting on the boat with his niece on his lap, was only giving Daisy's chatter half his attention. Because he couldn't get Rose out of his head. This was stupid. They tolerated each other, and only just. Besides, she wasn't his type. He liked sophisticated women who dressed in business suits and high heels. Women with sharp haircuts and sharp brains. Whereas Rose's hair made her look as if she'd just got out of bed; she dressed like a hippy in slip-dresses, lace and velvet; and she was definitely more likely to go barefoot than to wear high heels.

Brains… Hmm. That was where Rose puzzled him. The glance he'd taken at her business records told him she was neat and efficient. Bright. Which sat at odds with the fact he'd always considered her one of Sara's flakiest friends. She'd been a bit evasive about her work, too…

'Uncle Leo!'

His niece's imperious tone brought him back to the present. 'Sorry, honey.'

'Can we go to Aunty Rose's museum after we've seen the fairies?'

'Aunty Rose's museum?' What was she talking about?

'It's near the dinosaurs.' Daisy smiled. 'There's lots and lots of pretty clothes there.'

Dinosaurs. The Natural History Museum in Kensington? And if the museum was near there…did she mean the V and A? 'Why is it Aunty Rose's museum?'

''Cos she works there. Mummy and me see her there some-times.'

Hmm. Rose had said something about curators' jobs being thin on the ground. She definitely hadn't told him she worked at a museum. Even though he'd asked her outright. Why? 'Does she work there a lot?'

Daisy nodded. 'On Mondays, me and Mummy go to see her when I finish nursery. We go to the café and Aunty Rose gets me a special packed lunch. Sometimes it has a chocolate lolly in it.'

Yeah, and he'd bet Rose made her eat all her vegetables or fruit before she'd let Daisy eat the chocolate—just as well, because Sara was the sort who ate pudding first. But now his curiosity was piqued. 'What does Aunty Rose do at the museum?'

'Special sewing. And she puts clothes on people in glass cases.'

It sounded as if Rose did displays and conservation work part-time in a museum. Why hadn't she told him when he'd asked? Why had she let him think she didn't use her degree, that she'd just got a little market stall that was enough to make ends meet, that she was drifting along the same way his baby sister did?

'So can we?'

'If there's time. It's not that far from Kew.'

'Oh, goody. I can show you Aunty Rose's special glass cases.'

'I'd like that,' Leo said.

Daisy didn't manage to find any fairies at Kew. But then Leo promised her the same special lunch Aunty Rose gave her on Mondays, and they headed for the museum in Kensington.

'Look, these are Aunty Rose's,' Daisy said, tugging at his hand.

A display of clothes from the eighteen twenties. And there was a rack of leaflets next to it. Acting on a hunch, he skim-read one. It explained about the design and fabrics, about the way clothes were produced in the era. Whoever had written it clearly knew what he or she was talking about—and could explain in a way to make the reader just as enthusiastic.

And what interested him even more was the note at the bottom, telling him the author's name.

A certain R. Carter.

He managed to concentrate on his niece for the rest of the afternoon, but all the same he couldn't stop thinking about Rose. She was clever. And intelligence was something he'd always found a huge turn-on. A clever woman who could fence with him.

Ah, hell. Two days ago, he'd considered Rose Carter flaky, unreliable, and at about the same level as pondlife.

Now… He still thought she was a bit flaky. Different. Not

from his world. But she was organised, bright, and sexy as hell.
Which made her dangerous. The kind of woman who could
tempt him away from his focus. Someone he really should avoid.

Ah, hell. They didn't even *like* each other. But all the same
he wondered. Did she feel that same pull? Did she wonder what
it would be like to kiss him? Did she want to just forget the
outside world and make their own little world together...in a
four-poster bed with the curtains closed?

'Uncle Leo, you've got a really funny look on your face,'
Daisy said, tugging at his hand.

'Just thinking.' Lusting. And it had to stop right now. 'C'mon,
Princess. Time to make tracks for home.'

She nodded and tried to trot along beside him; even though he
slowed his pace to match hers, he noticed that she was flagging.

'You OK, Daisy?'

'My legs are tired,' she whispered, and there was the slightest pout to her lips.

He scooped her up. 'I'll carry you.'

'Thank you, Uncle Leo.' She curled her arms round his neck
and nestled against his chest. As he carried her out of the museum
his eye was caught by several women—all of whom had that soft
expression on their faces as they looked at him. A man carrying
a small child was a definite babe-magnet, he thought wryly. They
clearly had him pegged as a single father—a devoted dad taking
his daughter out for the day. And if he'd wanted to play on it, he
could probably have set himself up with half a dozen dates by
the time they got to South Kensington tube station.

But right now there was a face he couldn't get out of his head.
A face he really needed to get out of his head, for his sanity's sake.
A relationship with Rose would be a disaster. She'd distract him
from his career goals—and he really couldn't afford that. As the
eldest Ballantyne son and the one named after his grandfather,
Leo was expected to do well and match Leo the elder's record of
being one of the youngest ever QCs. He expected *himself* to do
that. He'd worked hard and he was right on target to succeed—
so he really didn't have time for this.

Though there was a little voice whispering inside his head.

Your life's an empty space, and you're filling it with your job.
There's something missing. Something important missing. And
she's the one who can help you find it.

His common sense knew better. For goodness' sake, he even
had a first-hand example! His godfather—Harry, Leo's father's
best friend—had fallen for someone who really didn't fit in with
the legal world. And in the legal world, if you wanted to get to
the top you had to marry the right person. Although Leo was extremely fond of his godmother, he'd always wondered if Harry
regretted the fact he'd never reached his full potential. That Harry
had never quite fitted in any more after his marriage to Natasha,
had always been overlooked for promotion.

OK, so it had been thirty-five years ago: but the legal world
moved extremely slowly. Things hadn't changed that much. A
would-be QC and a market trader. Nope. It didn't compute. If
Leo wanted to get to the top of his profession, Rose was just
about the worst person he could possibly pick as a girlfriend.
Which was why he was ever so slightly abrupt with her when she
met him back at Sara's flat. Why he concentrated his energies
on Daisy. Why he only picked at the pasta and garlic bread Rose
cooked for them all that evening.

He really ought to go home. He knew that Rose would look
after Daisy with as much care as he would. But he couldn't drag
himself away after he'd bathed Daisy. Hell. He wanted to be near
Rose—and he wanted to be a hundred miles away, at the same
time. His head and his heart were running in opposite directions.
And, for once in his life, he wasn't sure which one to follow.
They'd always gone together, before.

She'd clearly picked up on his mood, because she didn't try
to have a conversation with him. Just did her accounts, put her
books away, and started working on a garment. Leo, with an excellent vantage point on the sofa behind his newspaper, found
himself watching her. Watching the quick, deft way her fingers
worked. Watching the way she stroked the material.

Uh. He'd better start thinking of case law. Something dry and
dull. Something to get his body back to normal. Because
watching Rose made him wonder what those same fingers would

feel like working against his skin. Kneading. Stroking. Rubbing. Teasing. Making him hotter and hotter and hotter.

Why couldn't he tear his gaze away?

And he noticed that when she concentrated, her lips were very slightly parted. The lower lip full, sensual. It was just begging to be caught between his lips. Lord, he wanted to kiss her. Tease her mouth open so he could kiss her properly. Hot and wet and demanding. He wanted to feel her hands sliding through his hair—better still, across his bare skin. Better even than that, guiding him into her body.

Bad, bad, bad. He shouldn't even be thinking about getting naked with Rose Carter. He'd better go, before he did something they'd both regret. He was about to fold his newspaper away when the front door slammed and Sara bounced into the room.

'Hi, hi, hi, I've had a fabulous time and, Rose Carter, you are the bestest friend in the whole wide—' Sara stopped abruptly as she saw her brother sitting there. 'Oh. I didn't know you were going to be here.'

Leo scoffed. 'C'mon. You sent Mum a text with the sketch-iest of messages. You knew she'd panic and ring me.'

'And you'd come stomping over in a mood to boss me about.' Sara gave an exaggerated wince and hugged her best friend. 'I'm sorry, Rosie. I shouldn't've landed *him* on you.'

'It's OK. There hasn't been a problem,' Rose said quietly.

'Is Daze still up?' Sara asked hopefully.

'In bed. Asleep,' Leo informed her.

'I *need* to see her. It's been two days. Fifty hours.' Sara tugged at her hair. 'I missed her. She was asleep every time I phoned. Look, I won't wake her. I just want to see her beautiful little face.' She smiled at Rose. 'I loved every second at the spa. But not having Daze with me—it was like something was missing. My *baby*.'

She flitted out of the room, and Leo and Rose exchanged a glance.

'Don't rain on her parade,' Rose said softly.

'I wasn't going to.' Leo's eyes narrowed.

Uh-oh. She had a feeling he was reverting to type. Reverting to his position in the family: the oldest sibling, the one who bossed all the others about. 'I'll put the kettle on,' Rose said, and fled to the kitchen.

When she came back, Sara and Leo were looking daggers at each other.

'Um, I can see you two have stuff to sort out. I'll go,' Rose said, packing her mending away.

'Thanks for looking after Daisy for me. And for my birthday present. I *was* completely destressed,' Sara said, pointedly looking at her brother.

'Actually, I didn't do that much. Lizzy had food poisoning, so I had to man the stall. Leo looked after Daisy for me during the day.' Seeing her friend's face darken, Rose added swiftly, 'And they had a great time.'

Sara frowned. 'Oh, don't say he's got you on his side too, and you're going to start nagging me.'

'No. But maybe you two need to talk,' Rose said. 'Without fighting.' She hugged Sara. 'See you later.' Leo...well, they weren't on hugging terms. And she tried very hard not to mind. 'Bye, Leo.'

He nodded curtly; Rose gathered her things together and left.

The plan was, she'd go straight home. Except her car refused to start.

'Don't you give out on me now. I need to get home,' she informed the car.

Maybe she'd flooded the engine. She'd give it two minutes and try again.

Still no response.

OK. So she'd have to give in and call her car breakdown recovery service.

Except her mobile phone battery was flat.

'What is this, the day of all machinery giving up on me?' she asked in disbelief.

But it left her no choice. She'd have to go back to Sara's and use her phone. Hopefully Sara and Leo wouldn't be in the middle of a row...

Sara answered the door, looking faintly mutinous, but smiled when she saw Rose. 'Hiya. Forgotten something?'

'Car won't start.' Rose waved her phone at her. 'And this has got a flat battery. Can I borrow your phone and ring the break-down recovery people?'

'Sure you can. Unless my know-all brother can fix your car.'

'I'm not a know-all,' Leo said, appearing beside Sara. 'But, yes, I do know something about cars. What's the problem?'

'Won't start,' Rose said. She rubbed a hand across her face. Oh, great. Leo had reverted to type. Stuffy, disapproving, and he probably thought she was such a flake, she'd forgotten to put petrol in her car or something. 'I know how to top up the oil and water, fill it with petrol and check my own tyre pressures, but the garage deals with anything else.'

'I'll take a look,' Leo said.

Out of duty? No, thanks. 'It's OK. I'm sure you're busy. I'll call the recovery people.'

'I'll look first,' he said. 'It might be something where I can do a quick fix, and it'll save you having to wait for them to turn up.' He held out his hand. 'Keys?'

Taking over. Just as he'd done with Daisy, at first. She'd thought he'd mellowed a bit, last night and first thing this morning; clearly it had only been temporary.

'Keys,' Leo said again, this time looking irritated.

Not surprising. She'd been in a daydream. Belatedly, she remembered her manners. 'Uh—thanks.' She handed them over.

'Sara, do you own a torch?' he asked.

Sara scowled. 'I'm not *that* hopeless, Leo. Of course I do.' Though it took her ten minutes to find it. Ten minutes during which Rose didn't have a clue what to say to Leo, and he didn't make it easy for her either.

Funny how he'd changed. Yesterday, after his day out with Daisy, he'd seemed relaxed, almost carefree. This afternoon, he'd been in a strange mood. And now he was as starchy and un-approachable as he'd been on Friday night.

Finally, Sara appeared with the torch and Rose followed Leo back down to her car. He tried starting it; still, the engine refused to turn over. He climbed out of the driver's seat and put the bonnet up. 'Can you hold the torch for me?' he asked.

'Sure.' She trained the beam onto the engine.

He fiddled with some wires and various things she couldn't name, then looked at her.

'OK. Give it another try.'

She climbed in the driver's seat and turned the key. This time, the car started. 'Thanks,' she muttered. 'It'll get me home. I'll take it into the garage in the morning.'

'Good idea.' But just as she was about to drive off, he held up a hand. 'Hang on. I'll follow you home. Just in case it cuts out. Don't turn the engine off—leave it ticking over. I'll just say goodbye to Sara.'

A very brief goodbye, and Rose guessed it hadn't been that amicable because he was frowning as he reached her car. 'OK. I'm parked not far behind you. I'll pull out first, then let you out in front of me.'

'Look, I'm probably miles out of your way. I'll be fine.'

'It's not a big deal. Don't make it one,' Leo said. 'I'll follow you.'

For a second, Rose was tempted to rebel and drive off before he even got into his car. Then common sense prevailed. If her car broke down at a traffic light or junction, it would be awkward. And, with her mobile phone needing to be charged up so she couldn't ring for help, it was only sensible to let Leo act as her safety net.

He flashed his headlights at her to let her know he was ready, and she pulled out. Drove home—to her relief, the car made it—and parked on the street outside her flat.

Leo parked immediately behind her and got out of his car.

'Thanks for seeing me home,' she said.

'No problem.'

He sounded a bit abrupt, but it was more or less what she'd been expecting. So she thought it was safe to be polite and ask him, 'Um, would you like to come in for a coffee?'

He looked at her for a moment. Just as she'd expected, he was going to be just as polite and refuse. *Thanks, but I'm busy.*

'Thanks.'

And then he really shocked her by saying, 'That'd be nice.'

CHAPTER FIVE

No. Leo had meant to say no. He was supposed to be giving this woman a wide berth. He'd only offered to follow her home for Sara's sake—out of a sense of responsibility, really, to make sure her friend was safe and Sara wouldn't worry about her. He didn't want to have coffee with her or socialise with her in any way.

Ha. Who was he trying to kid? His head might want to avoid her, but his heart wanted to know what made Rose tick. What her inner sanctum was like. The outside was an Edwardian block in Camden—well, it figured that she'd choose an older property, unlike his sparkling new penthouse in Clerkenwell. He already knew she liked vintage things.

And she was about to fall backwards down the stairs, if she wasn't careful; no way could she see where she was going. 'Let me take those boxes,' he said.

She was reluctant to give them up. 'I normally manage them perfectly well on my own.'

Independent, too. And clearly didn't know when to stop. 'You'll need at least one hand free to unlock the door.' He stopped the argument simply by lifting the boxes from her and shouldering the load himself.

Rose's mouth compressed—obviously she was annoyed at the way he'd just taken over—but she led him up to the second floor. Opened the door and switched on the light. 'Come in. Take a seat.'

'Where do you want the boxes?'

'Just here by the door will do, thanks.'

He put the boxes down, then looked around him. He wasn't

sure what he'd expected, but this place suited Rose perfectly. Rich colours and textures everywhere. The windows were large sash windows with cream damask drapes and soft muslin nets; the walls were painted old gold; and the parquet flooring had several rugs dotted carelessly on it, the rich jewel tones picking out the ruby colour of the overstuffed sofa and the dark sapphire velvet cushions.

And the room was immaculately tidy. A far cry from Sara's chaotic surroundings.

There was a small table in one corner that housed a laptop; underneath was a clear plastic lidded box full of files, which he had a hunch would be neatly labelled and grouped in alphabetical order, and another clear plastic lidded box which seemed to be full of toys. Probably for Daisy, he guessed. In the other corner there was a television and DVD player, with a decent stereo; behind the sofa was a wall full of shelves.

'Make yourself at home,' Rose said, switching on two lamps and flicking off the overhead light; she disappeared through the door to what he imagined was her kitchen.

He browsed along the shelves. A few romantic comedy paperbacks, books on the history of fashion and textiles, a stack of costume dramas on DVD—no surprises there. Little painted glass or exquisitely enamelled boxes were dotted here and there; he couldn't resist picking them up and examining them. Clearly this was something Rose collected; he assumed that some of them were antique, though several looked very modern.

There was a framed sampler on one wall, dating from eighteen sixty-two. Rose Smith. A distant relative, or just coincidence with the first name? There were also some beautiful line drawings, though the scribbled signatures were illegible. Rose's work? No, he had a feeling that Rose Carter would have a neat, precise signature. And she'd said she worked mainly with textiles.

There were photographs on the mantelpiece in pretty enamelled frames: a couple that were clearly her parents, because Rose had inherited her father's dark blue eyes and dark hair, and her mother's corkscrew curls. A picture of Rose with two men who looked enough like her to be her brothers. And one of Rose with Sara and Daisy, out having a picnic somewhere.

Who'd taken it? he wondered. Rose's boyfriend?

Then again, he couldn't see a photo of anyone who might fit into the category of 'boyfriend.' And it shocked him how pleased he was to think that. It shouldn't matter to him who Rose saw. He wasn't involved with her. Wasn't going to be involved with her, either. She was just Sara's irritating, flaky friend. She meant nothing to him. And having the hots for her wasn't anywhere near good enough reason to stray from the path he'd set himself.

He moved on to look at a framed pencil sketch of Daisy; he peered more closely at it and recognised his sister's signature on the sketch.

'Yes, it's one of Sara's,' Rose said, reappearing with two mugs. She handed one to him, then sat down on the furthest chair away from him.

Running scared? Hmm. He didn't think Rose was scared of men. She must deal with them all the time at work. So why was she avoiding contact with him? Did she feel the same odd tension between them? Did it unnerve her as much as it unnerved him?

'It's a nice room,' he offered, taking a seat on the sofa and cupping his hands round his mug.

'Thanks.'

'Very you.'

She raised an eyebrow at that, as if to say he didn't have a clue about her. 'Not what you expected?'

'Well, no,' he admitted. 'I expected there to be clothes everywhere.' He'd expected the place to be a mess. Full of incense and flaky stuff. Whereas the only things in evidence that could be described as flaky were a couple of candles in wrought iron holders—things you'd see in just about any house.

She smiled. 'I have a cupboard and a rail for my stock. I need to store them properly, because customers aren't going to buy crumpled clothes. They want something they can wear, not something they have to launder and iron first. Especially as vintage fabrics often need to be hand-washed.'

'Good point.' He gestured to the line drawings. 'Are the rest of those sketches Sara's, too? Or yours?'

'Neither. Friends from art college.'

'Uh-huh.' He paused, and gestured to her mug. 'You're not having coffee?'

'I gave it up some time ago. It gives me headaches.'

Probably the caffeine. 'Ever tried decaffeinated?'

She pulled a face. 'It's like alcohol-free wine or low-fat ice cream. A poor substitute that just doesn't taste right.' She shrugged. 'So I drink orange and cinnamon tea, and keep the real stuff for friends and visitors.'

He noted the distinction, and knew he was definitely in the latter category, in her eyes. Though he'd rather be in the former.

Actually, he'd rather be in a completely different category. *Lover.* Something that would give him the right to set his coffee down, go over to her chair, pick her up and tumble her onto the sofa. See her hair fanning out, silk against the velvet. Kiss her until all the tension in the room melted away.

He swallowed hard. Hell. The more time he spent with her, the more he wanted her. This was crazy. Stupid. Lust, that was all it was. A temporary attraction. He'd come to his senses any second now.

Any second now.

The silence stretched between them. Just when he thought it would crack, Rose put down her mug of fruit tea and switched on the stereo.

OK. So this was where he'd have to sit through new-age stuff. The kind of stuff Sara played to irritate him. The kind of stuff that would definitely drive him out of her flat.

But the music Rose played was nothing like that. A soft, haunting saxophone filled the air, together with a pure, clear alto. Goose-bumps rippled his flesh. 'What's this?' he asked quietly.

She handed him the CD box so he could see the details for himself. 'It's actually a Breton carol, but I can imagine this being used in a film.' Her face took on a dreamy expression. 'Something medieval. A quest film, where they're walking through a very spooky forest in the middle of winter. Or maybe a highwayman being marched to the gallows.'

He could imagine it, too. 'This is... Wow.'

'You were expecting whale music, weren't you?' There was a definite glitter of amusement in her eyes.

'Well...yeah,' he admitted. 'The sort of stuff Sara plays.'

The corner of her mouth quirked. 'The sort of stuff she plays when she wants to get rid of people. Most of the time she plays pop, the kind of tunes you can sing to.'

Why had he never realised that? Probably, he thought, because usually Sara wanted to get rid of him. 'I see.' He hadn't made it over to the small stack of CDs by Rose's stereo, so he had no idea what she listened to. But a nasty suspicion hit him. Was this haunting stuff the sort of thing she played when *she* wanted to get rid of people? Spook them away?

Either it was obvious in his expression or he'd unwittingly spoken the question aloud, because she smiled. 'Most of the time I listen to ballads from the fifties. Nat King Cole, Julie London, stuff like that. But a friend played me this the other day. I liked it, so I bought it.'

Impulsive. Yes, that was Rose. She'd do things on a whim. She wouldn't plan, as he did. She'd go out to buy bread and come back with an armful of irises. It would drive him crazy. No way was it ever going to work between them. He shouldn't even be thinking about it. In fact, he should go. Right now.

So why the hell wasn't he standing up and thanking her politely for the coffee and leaving? Why was he still here, wanting to be near her?

Leo looked like a man at war with himself. Rose was sure that, underneath his starchy exterior, there was someone more interesting trying to get out. Someone who'd maybe forgive the odd imperfection.

Though what she'd seen of Leo made her realise he wanted to be perfect. To excel. To be the best at what he did. Then she caught herself speculating what Leo would be like at kissing. Making love. Would he be focused and intense, striving for perfection there too?

Um. Absolutely not what she should be thinking about. Especially with the man himself sitting only a few feet away.

Then she realised that he'd been talking to her.

'Sorry. I missed that,' she admitted.

'I was saying, you look tired.'

She seized the let-out gratefully. 'I am, a bit.'

'Then I'll go.' He drained his coffee. 'Thank you for the drink.'

'Thank you for seeing me home.'

And this was how it would all end. Being polite to each other. Distant strangers. She stood up and took the mug from him, ready to show him out.

Then he said something completely unexpected. 'Rose. I'd like to see you.'

'What?'

'I'd like to see you,' he repeated. 'Have dinner with me tomorrow night.'

Leo was asking her out? Or was she hallucinating? Had she fallen asleep and her dreams were full of wishful thinking?

But she'd already learned her lesson the hard way. Relationships equalled a lot more hassle than they were worth. 'Thanks, but no.'

'Why?'

Trust Leo not to leave it there. Hadn't he already warned her that he usually got his own way? 'Because I don't date.'

'Neither do I.'

Her eyes narrowed. 'You just asked me out to dinner. That counts as a date.'

'We could pretend it wasn't.'

She blinked. 'This is surreal.'

'Why?'

'You and I—we don't even like each other.'

'Maybe we do. Maybe we just don't know each other...yet.'

She shook her head. 'It's a bad idea. I don't date.' Not after Steve. If your judgement in men was lousy, the simplest way to avoid a bad situation was not to date. Ever. She dragged in a breath. 'I like my life as it is. Uncomplicated.'

'Just your work, your friends and your family.' He shrugged. 'Me too.'

'So why did you ask me?'

'Because.' He sighed. 'Because...of this.'

Before she realised what he had in mind, he cupped her face with both hands and brushed his mouth against hers. The lightest, softest, gentlest touch. Unthreatening. Not even the faintest scratch from his stubble.

Then he did it again, and her mouth tingled. She wanted to run her tongue over her lower lip, but no way was she going to do something so obvious. Then her body stopped listening to her mind and her lips parted slightly, inviting another kiss.

'I've wanted to do that ever since Friday night,' he said. 'When you were wearing that feather boa. And I could just imagine...' He dropped his hands from her face.

His eyes had darkened, just as she'd known they would. And his mouth... Why hadn't she noticed just how beautiful his mouth was? Even white teeth. A full lower lip. A sensual smile that promised all kinds of pleasures.

'Rose.' His voice was husky, full of desire. Like a spell, binding her so she couldn't think of anything else but him. How long his eyelashes were. She wanted to reach out and touch them. Let her fingertips skate over his skin, roughened by the stubble. Trace the soft, soft curve of his lower lip. Feel him suck the tip of her forefinger into his mouth.

Thank God she was holding the mugs and couldn't do it.

But it was almost as if he could read her mind, because she heard a clink and realised that he'd taken them from her. Put them on a shelf.

This time, he wound his fingers through her hair. 'I knew it'd be this soft.' He played with her curls. 'You look like a Celtic faery who's come to bewitch me.'

'They had green eyes,' she corrected automatically. 'Not blue.'

'Not necessarily. What about Etain? "Eyes as blue as the dark hyacinth, lips as red as the berries of the rowan tree."'

'Etain?'

'From Celtic mythology. The Irish bardic romances. She was the goddess of the sun. Now I think of it, she had golden hair. Though your hair's beautiful.' He let her hair trail through his fingers, then rubbed his thumb along her lower lip. 'She was married to the god Midir.'

But…Leo was a barrister. A workaholic who was steeped in the law. How would he know Celtic mythology?

She must have asked it, not thought it, because he gave her the full-wattage smile. 'Used to read a lot when I was in my late teens. Lots of obscure stuff.'

'Oh.' Well, he would. He probably spoke half a dozen languages fluently as well, and could do Japanese number-puzzles in about thirty seconds flat. Leo was a Renaissance man. Polymath. Good at everything.

And, oh, he'd be a master at making love.

Uh. She had to stop thinking about that. It wasn't going to happen—and if she didn't get it out of her head right now she'd spontaneously combust.

He traced her upper lip with his forefinger. 'Rose. I need to kiss you.'

She should take a step back. Tell him no. She knew that. So how come her arms were round his neck and her fingers were threading through his hair? How come her mouth was opening under his? How come her breasts felt heavy and full and her nipples had gone incredibly sensitive and she ached for him to touch them?

For someone who claimed he didn't date, Leo sure as hell knew a lot about kissing. About how to tease her mouth until she was practically panting. Tiny, nibbling kisses, promising and demanding at the same time.

And then his tongue slid into her mouth. Exploring. Tasting. Inciting her to kiss him back. What could she do but respond?

He had one hand curved over her bottom and the other flat against her spine, pressing her to him. Hard muscle against the softness of her breasts, flat abdomen against the curve of her belly. And she could feel his erection pressing against her, too; he was definitely as turned on as she was. Wanting this. Needing this.

Somehow, he'd lifted her. Cupped her buttocks in both hands. Spun her round so her back was against the door. Her legs were wrapped round him—how, when she had no memory of doing it?—and his sex was pressed against hers, their clothes the only barrier between them.

He tilted his hips, just once, very slowly, so she could feel just how turned on he was. If he hadn't been kissing her, she would have moaned aloud. But the sound was lost in his mouth, which had grown more demanding now. Sucking and nipping. Tasting and exploring. Pushing her to the point where she was going to throw everything to the wind and say yes. Where she'd take him to her bed and to hell with tomorrow.

And then he stopped. Stared at her. 'Rose,' he whispered.

His mouth was red. Swollen. As if they'd been kissing for hours. No doubt hers was in the same state.

She had no idea how long they'd been kissing. Minutes? Hours? Days? Whatever. Time had just stopped. All she'd been aware of was his mouth. His taste. The feel of his skin against hers.

'It's going to happen.' His voice was husky, but very, very sure. He let her slide downwards until her feet were touching the floor again—making very sure that her body was in contact with his, the whole way. 'Not tonight, but it's going to happen.'

She opened her mouth to say, 'Not in a million years,' but no sound came out.

'Rose.' He rubbed his thumb along her lower lip. 'There's a spark between us.'

'No, there isn't.' Spark? More like a raging inferno. Not good. Not what she needed in her life—not now, not ever.

Just when she'd geared herself up for a battle, he stroked her hair. Gentle. Soothing her. Undermining her defences. 'What's the problem?' he asked.

The fact that her judgement in men was lousy, for starters. Not that she could tell Leo that. He was a lawyer. He made his living arguing niceties. If she tried to argue with him, she'd lose.

She couldn't *afford* to lose. No way was she going to put herself in that position again. Getting involved, tying up her life with someone else's, seeing everything fall apart and having to build it all up from the rubble again—absolutely not. It had been hard enough last time. Next time, she might not have the strength to do it. Best to keep as she was. Single, fulfilled and happy.

She refused to meet his eyes. 'We're from different worlds. As I said before, we don't even like each other.'

He nodded. 'I didn't like the person I thought you were. But you're not that person.' He rubbed the tip of his nose against hers. 'I'm man enough to admit I got you wrong. Are you woman enough to admit maybe you've got me wrong?'

'I…' Oh, God. Just when she'd thought she knew what she was doing, he made her think again.

I'm man enough.

He wasn't being deliberately smutty—she was sure he wasn't. But all she could think about was the fact he was a man. All man. A very aroused man. A very sexy, aroused man. She needed to put some space between them. Fast. But how could she, with her back to the door and his body only a millimetre away from hers—not touching, not threatening, but promising, tempting, inciting her to close that gap herself?

'Think about it.' He brushed his mouth against hers. 'Or maybe—don't think about it. Listen to what your body's telling you.'

The material of her top was thin and her nipples were hard, so her arousal would be very obvious to him. And her body was saying something completely different from what her mind was shrieking. *All systems go,* instead of *definitely no.* She dragged in a breath. 'That's—that's just lust.' Lust on a scale she'd never experienced before. 'Transient,' she added, while she could still manage coherent speech. If he moved forward a single millimetre, crossed that last bit of distance between them so her breasts rubbed against his chest, she'd be babbling. Worse, she had a feeling she'd be ripping his clothes off and begging him to take her right there and then.

'Transient?' His eyes crinkled at the corners. 'It's not going to be transient, Rose. It's going to take a lot, lot longer than you think.'

Oh, the images *that* set flickering in her brain. She was going to hyperventilate. Or spontaneously combust.

'All night,' he murmured, looking her straight in the eye.

She was very, very glad that she was leaning against the door. Otherwise she would definitely have slid to the floor. Boneless.

'And soon.' He brushed his mouth over hers again. 'I'm leaving now. While I still can. But I'll call you.' Another nibble.

'Or you can call me.' One more kiss, and he'd gently moved her away from the door. Saw himself out.

And Rose stared at the closed door, feeling as if she'd just been flattened by a typhoon.

CHAPTER SIX

'LEO, Mr Lane's been on the line again.' Jessie, Leo's clerk, leaned round the door. 'He's insistent that he needs to speak to you.'

'To me?' Leo frowned.

'Yes. You know, in connection with the big case that's going to court next month.'

Yeah, he knew the case.

'He's already called you four times this morning.' She stared at him. 'Are you all right?'

'I'm fine.'

'You did ring him…?' Her voice trailed off; clearly his expression told her that, no, he hadn't returned the calls.

Because he'd been distracted.

Because he'd been thinking about something other than his job.

Which he could only do here, in his office—if he'd been in court today and not been concentrating a hundred per cent on what he was doing, it would've been a complete nightmare. He'd have lost his case for sure. His grandfather would have been disgusted by the way Leo was disgracing the family name. Leo could even see the old man's disdainful shake of the head in his mind's eye. Hear the contempt in his voice. 'Just like your father. Full of promise but never lived up to it. Call yourself a Ballantyne?'

If he carried on like this, he'd never make QC.

Hell, hell, hell. He had to focus.

'Are you sure you're all right?' Jessie asked.

'I'm fine. Thank you,' he added belatedly.

'It's just…you seem a bit…distracted.'

She could say that again. His mind had been playing that kiss on continuous loop. To the point where he was going crazy. 'Absolutely not,' Leo said curtly. 'I'll call him now.'

'Ow!' Rose stuck her forefinger in her mouth and sucked it. When was the last time she'd pricked herself? And to do it when she was in the middle of conservation work was just stupid. She needed to concentrate on what she was doing, and she really didn't need to have to clean specks of blood from the fine cream woollen dress she was working on.

It would be easier if she weren't thinking of a pair of grey eyes. Sexy grey eyes. Grey eyes that had darkened with desire as he'd lifted her and pressed his body against hers and—

'Ow, ow, *ow!*' This time the needle had gone in really deeply. Scowling, Rose sucked the blood from the pinprick, left her work where it was, and headed to get a plaster.

Pity the first-aid kit didn't contain something for keeping clever, stuffy, but sexy-as-hell barristers out of your head.

Leo needed some fresh air. Right now. To blow thoughts of Rose out of his head. For once he'd take a lunch break—a twenty-minute walk might help him focus again. He was passing the open door of the clerks' room when he heard his name.

'Leo's really not himself today.'

Even knowing that eavesdroppers never heard anything nice about themselves, he couldn't resist pausing. Waiting to see what his clerk said.

'Reckon he's going down with some virus?'

He recognised that voice, too. Stella, the receptionist. The biggest gossip in the building. Not good.

'No, I reckon it's a woman.' Jessie lowered her voice, though Leo could still hear her. 'And she must be something really special, to distract the biggest workaholic in the whole of Lincoln's Inn.'

Workaholic? He wasn't a workaholic. He just saw what needed to be done, and did it. In less time than it would take most other people, too.

'Is it someone here?' Stella asked.

'Dunno,' Jessie said thoughtfully. 'Clare's a bit mousy, not his type. He likes confident women. Bright ones. Ones who dress a bit more…well, sharper than Clare.'

Jessie and Stella were trying to fix him up with *Clare*? He liked the junior barrister, but he'd only ever seen her as a colleague. She didn't set his world on fire.

He pushed aside the thought that Rose could.

And since when had his clerk had a handle on exactly what he liked in women, anyway?

'What about Rebecca?' Stella suggested.

'Yes, it could be.'

Rebecca worked in a different set of chambers, in the floor above his. She was easily the most stunning-looking woman in the whole building—bright, too. Sophisticated. Could hold her own in any company. Perfect potential QC's wife—in fact, she'd be a QC herself, in the future. That was obvious.

Though Rebecca also happened to be a man-eater. Not Leo's type at all. He preferred his women a little softer. Subtler. Warmer.

He blew out a breath. He needed to stop the speculation before his clerk started being convinced that he was working his way through the married women in chambers. The last thing he needed right now was gossip. Gossip that would quickly reach the ears of the head of chambers and start putting question marks over Leo's suitability for promotion. Over his suitability to become a QC.

'In case anyone needs to know where I am, I'm taking a lunch break,' he said, putting his head round the door of the clerks' room.

'Lunch break?'

Oh, hell. The speculation in Stella's eyes doubled. Because Leo never took lunch breaks when he was in the office—he had a sandwich delivered to his desk and worked right through. If he was in court, lunch usually meant a working lunch—a meeting with the solicitor working on his case team.

The fact that he was going out…oh, no. Now they were going to start thinking he was having a clandestine meeting with some woman or other.

He didn't owe them any kind of explanation. But somehow he found himself saying, 'I read an interesting article in the Sunday papers. About how taking a ten-minute walk at lunchtime can improve your focus.' True, and he'd dismissed it. In his view, lunch was for people who didn't have enough stamina. 'So today's an experiment. I'll be back in half an hour.'

Jessie did at least have the grace to look the teeniest bit embarrassed, clearly realising he'd overheard them talking. Though Stella was completely brazen about it. He didn't bother chastising her; he already knew she was a lost cause.

'Oh, and just so you're both completely up to date with the latest gossip, I'm not seeing anyone. At all,' he in-formed them.

Which was true. He wasn't seeing Rose Carter.

And he tried to ignore the little word that slid into his head. *Yet.*

Leo managed to stay focused for the rest of the day; but when his laptop beeped—the reminder he'd set so he'd remember to call Sara at a reasonable time—he paused for a moment. Everywhere was silent. Clearly he was the last one left in chambers.

Maybe his clerk was right. He was a workaholic. But he had a lot to live up to. And if he wanted to make the grade, he had to put in the hours. Show he was prepared to work hard. Prove himself.

He scowled. There was absolutely nothing wrong with being dedicated to your job. And no reason at all to think of the slightly pitying look on Jessie's face when he'd declared that he wasn't seeing anyone.

He picked up his mobile phone. For a second, he almost called Rose. Then common sense kicked in, and instead he speed-dialled his sister's number. The answering machine clicked in; either she was giving Daisy a bath, reading her a story, or just couldn't be bothered to answer the phone. The latter was more likely. 'Hello, Sara. It's Leo. Just ringing to see if you're OK.'

Or maybe Sara was busy chatting to Rose.

No. He wasn't going to think about Rose. He wasn't going to chase her. She had his number—and phone connections worked both ways. If she wanted to see him, she'd call him.

'Give Daisy a kiss for me. I'll call you later in the week. Ring me if you need anything.' He suppressed the thought that Sara never rang him just for a chat, that she found him too unapproachable. He was busy and she respected it, that was all. He cut the connection, glanced at his watch, and decided to work for just another hour.

He managed to hold out until Wednesday night. Another night when he'd worked so late that he was the last in the building.

And then he called Rose.

'Hello?'

She sounded faintly wary. Clearly his name had shown up on the screen of her phone. That, or she'd remembered his number. Or maybe she was just wary anyway. 'Hello, Rose. It's Leo.'

'Is something wrong with Sara or Daisy?'

An obvious question. Why else would he be ringing her? 'No.'

'Good.'

Lord, she had a lovely voice. No discernible accent. But thinking of her voice made him think about her mouth. Bad move. Because he wanted to feel her mouth against his again. Wanted to feel her lips against his throat. Wanted to feel her mouth slowly arrowing down his body, until it closed round—

Oh-h-h.

'Have you eaten?' he asked, trying to keep his voice as normal as possible. God, he hoped he didn't sound as if he were practically panting down the phone. Even though he was.

'It's eight o'clock, Leo.'

So it was. She was bound to have eaten already. No point in asking her to have dinner with him tonight, then. 'Can I call in to see you on my way home tonight?'

'I'm not on your way home.'

'You are if I take the scenic route.'

She chuckled wryly. 'You've got an answer for everything.'

He laughed back. 'Of course I have. That's why I'm a barrister.'

'A good one.'

Ouch. If he said yes, he'd sound boastful—even though it happened to be true. He didn't want her to think he was some pompous oaf. But if he said no, he'd sound falsely modest and patronising—which was just as bad. He went for the middle course. 'I do OK. So. See you in about forty minutes?'

'I...' A soft sigh. 'OK.'

Forty minutes. He was going to be here in forty minutes. Rose wrapped her arms tightly round herself. What ever had possessed her to say yes? This was a bad idea. Every way she looked at it, this was a bad idea. Her past relationships had all been disasters and she'd ended up hurt. Especially the last time. Plus she and Leo were from different worlds: Leo thought she was flaky at best, a criminal at worst, and she already knew firsthand that she didn't fit into the law community.

So when he got here, she'd explain very politely that this was a bad idea. She'd show him out and that would be that.

By the time her intercom bleeped, Rose's knuckles were white and her heart felt as if it were beating twice as fast as normal. She took a deep breath and pressed the button.

'Hello, Rose. It's Leo.'

'Come up.' She pressed the button again to let him in.

He was wearing a suit again. Well, he would be—he'd spent the day in chambers. And he looked drop-dead gorgeous in it...but remote. Untouchable. As he'd been that Friday night. Nowhere near as dangerous as he looked when he needed a shave and was wearing casual clothes.

And at least he hadn't brought her flowers, so she wouldn't feel guilty about telling him to go. She took a deep breath, ready to explain that this was a bad idea. But her mouth clearly wasn't listening to her brain, because completely different words came out. 'Have you eaten?' The same question he'd asked her. Because obviously when he'd called her he hadn't eaten, and he'd spent the time since then travelling from Lincoln's Inn to Camden. He wouldn't have had time even to grab a sandwich.

He shrugged. 'I'm not really that hungry.'

His eyes were saying something else. That he was hungry. *Very* hungry.

For her.

'You ought to eat properly. Look after yourself.'

His mouth quirked. 'Lecturing? Isn't that supposed to be my role?'

She flushed. 'Um.'

'But I'd do anything for a coffee,' he added. 'Please.'

'Uh-huh. Make yourself at home.'

Damn. Her mouth still wasn't in contact with her brain. Hello? Aren't you supposed to be explaining to Leo why this has to stop right now? Why you're not going to see each other again after tonight?

Her flat seemed much, much smaller with him in it. So did her galley kitchen, with him lounging against the worktop as she made him a coffee and herself a fruit tea. He was supposed to be sitting politely on the sofa, not invading her space and getting way too close for her personal comfort.

'There isn't really enough room for two people in here,' she said, hoping he'd get the hint.

Instead, he clearly took it that she was apologising for the narrowness of the room. 'It's charming. I like the colour scheme.' Painted white tongue-and-groove doors, aquamarine colour-washed walls, and a grey marble-effect worktop. 'It's light and fresh.'

'Thanks.'

A hint of amusement crept into his eyes as he accepted the mug of coffee from her and took a sip. 'Why do I make you so uncomfortable, Rose?'

'You don't,' she lied.

'You're fidgeting,' he observed. 'And you've put as much space as you possibly can between us.' He tipped his head slightly to one side. 'Supposing I took a step forward?' He set his mug on the worktop and closed the gap between them. Not completely. But so that he was near enough to touch her, if he reached out.

She dragged in a breath.

'See?' he said. 'And if I were to do this…' He reached out and gently took her mug from her. Set it on the worktop next to his.

Uh. When his fingers touched hers—even though it was a non-sexual, unthreatening touch—it felt as if a thousand volts had just zapped through her.

'Your eyes have just gone darker,' he said. 'And you just licked your bottom lip.'

Had she? She didn't remember doing that. But when she lifted a finger to her lips to check, she realised that he was right. Her lip was wet.

'I…Leo, I don't do relationships.'

'That's OK. Neither do I.' He reached out again, this time to touch her face. Cupping it in one hand. Rubbing his thumb gently against her skin, as if to reassure her that everything was going to be OK.

'I don't do affairs, either.' The words came out as a husky whisper.

'Neither do I.' His eyes, too, had darkened. And she noticed that they were fixed on her mouth.

He was going to kiss her.

Just as he'd kissed her on Sunday night.

When he'd lifted her up against the wall and her body had just melted against him and her brain had blown a few fuses.

'But maybe we should,' he said. 'Maybe we should just have a wild, wild affair and get this out of our systems.'

'There's nothing to get out of my system.'

He lifted an eyebrow. 'Isn't there?'

Then his hand slid from her face to the back of her neck, tugging her towards him.

'I think,' he whispered against her mouth, 'this is the same for you as it is for me.' He kissed the tip of her nose. 'Something you didn't expect.' Another kiss, this time at the corner of her mouth. 'Something that's messing with your head.' He brushed his lips against the other corner of her mouth. 'Something you really don't have time for—something you don't want in your life right now.' He pulled back very slightly, so she could meet his gaze. See how serious he was. 'But there's nothing either of us can do about it. It's there. I haven't stopped thinking about you all week, Rose. Every time I breathed in, I could smell your perfume. Every time I opened my mouth, I remembered the taste of you on my lips. I forgot to return phone calls on Monday—and I never forget anything.'

'I pricked my finger on Monday,' she admitted. 'Twice. And I never, ever prick myself when I'm working.'

'But you couldn't concentrate. Because you were thinking of me?' he asked.

'Yeah,' she said on a sigh.

'Which hand?'

'Doesn't matter now. It's healed.'

'Which hand?'

She lifted her left hand.

Still keeping his eyes on hers, he took her hand and lifted it to his mouth. Kissed it lightly. 'Just making it better,' he said huskily.

Desire snaked down her spine. Oh, Lord. What it would be to have that beautiful mouth touching her more intimately. Tracking up to the pulse hammering in her wrist. To the sensitive spot on her inner elbow. Up her arm, her shoulder. And then down again as he peeled her dress from her, let it fall to the floor in a puddle of silk. Kissing. Sucking. Drawing one nipple into his mouth.

As if he could guess her thoughts, he drew her forefinger into his mouth and sucked it, still looking into her eyes.

Her nipples tingled, and she could feel a pulse beating hard between her legs. Feel herself growing wet. Wanting him. Wanting more.

Her breath hitched as she remembered how he'd kissed her on Sunday night. Thought of just how strong his muscles were. How easy he'd find it to lift her onto the worktop and—

He released her hand. Smiled. 'Have dinner with me tomorrow night.'

Yes.

Except it wouldn't be just dinner, and they both knew it.

Part of her wanted to throw caution to the winds. But last time she'd done that, her life had been torn apart in the wreckage. She couldn't risk it again. 'I can't.'

'Can't, or won't?'

'Either. Both,' she admitted.

'It isn't any easier for me.'

'Isn't it?'

'No.' He looked serious, intense. Soul-destroyingly beautiful.

'It's not easy for me,' he said. 'Not at all. I want to take silk—become a QC,' he explained. 'I want to do what my grandfather did, become one of the youngest ever QCs. So I have to focus on my work. Be the best in my field. I can't let myself get distracted. I haven't got *time* for a relationship. I can't give a woman the attention she deserves. Except...' He rubbed his thumb against her lower lip. 'You're in my head, Rose. I'm working on a case, and suddenly all I can think about is you. Hear your voice. Smell your scent. Feel your mouth on mine. And it's not enough. Nowhere near enough. I want you so badly, it's driving me crazy.' A corner of his mouth lifted. 'I do hope you're not a mind-reader. Because what's going through my head right now would definitely get my face slapped.'

'We're going to be sensible about this. Walk away. Pretend it's not happening,' Rose said.

'Are we?' He leaned forward and touched his mouth to hers. Just the lightest, gentlest contact.

And the next thing she knew, her hands were in his hair, and he'd lifted her onto the kitchen work-surface and was standing between her thighs. Nudging against her. His hands were resting lightly on her waist, and she burned for them to touch her more intimately. To slide under the hem of her dress and skim over her thighs. To caress the soft, soft skin, tease her a little. Make her wriggle and tilt her hips, giving him better access. Cup her sex through her knickers and feel just how hot she was for him. Press a little harder, watch her gasp and tip her head back, offering her throat to him.

Oh-h-h.

If he didn't touch her, she was going to do something stupid—like beg.

If he *did* touch her, she was going to do something stupid—like beg.

How the hell had this man tipped her life upside down so fast? She wasn't sure if she was more scared or excited. Just that she wanted him. Needed him.

Now.

'See?' he asked softly. 'Just one touch, and we're both lost. We both react in a way our heads would normally say no to. It's *there*.'

Her head was swimming. She couldn't think clearly enough to speak—didn't trust herself to speak. She counted backwards from ninety-four—in sevens. And then she couldn't help sliding her hands down the arms of his suit. She'd wanted to touch the fabric for ages. She wanted to touch his skin even more, but the fabric would do. For now. 'Silk and wool blend. Nice.'

'Name the percentage,' he challenged.

She did.

'Spot on.' He looked impressed. 'Very good.'

She shrugged. 'It's what I do. Fabric.'

'So how are you on skin?' he asked.

Just what she'd been thinking. Wanting. She shivered. 'Leo. This isn't fair.'

'You're telling me. I can't get you out of my head, Rose. And—correct me if I'm wrong—I think it's the same for you.'

'Yes.'

'So either we go crazy, or we do something about it.'

Was he giving her a choice?

'You're a man of words.'

'And action.' His gaze met hers. Very clear, very direct. Grey eyes that were like quicksilver, molten with desire.

And, Lord, his mouth. His beautiful, beautiful mouth. She needed to feel his mouth against her skin. Right now.

So she said nothing. Didn't tell him to stop. Didn't tell him to leave.

He inclined his head, very slightly, just once; then warm air whispered against her skin as he lowered the zip of her dress. Slid the silk off her shoulders, down her arms—and slid her bra straps down at the same time.

'Stunning,' he breathed, and lowered his head. His mouth moved over her shoulders, across her collar-bones, and she closed her eyes, sliding her hands back into his hair.

This was crazy. They really shouldn't be doing this. She didn't do relationships—and she didn't do one-night stands either. But then she stopped thinking entirely as Leo unsnapped her bra and let the lacy garment fall into her lap. His hands cupped her breasts, lifting them; his thumbs rubbed against her already erect nipples. The friction felt so good, she inhaled sharply. Oh, yes.

But she still wanted more.

'So very, very beautiful,' he whispered against her skin.

And Rose almost came when he drew one nipple into his mouth. Sucked. 'Leo…'

It came out as a sob, and he stopped instantly. Restored order to her clothes. Laced his fingers through hers and brought them up to his mouth. 'I'm sorry. I got…carried away.' There was a dark slash of colour across his cheekbones. 'I shouldn't have done that.'

She hadn't exactly told him no, had she? She'd even arched her back to give him better access to her breasts. Ah, hell. 'We shouldn't,' she corrected.

He picked up on her words instantly. 'You were there with me. All the way.'

Yes. She felt her face flood with guilty colour. 'That wasn't supposed to happen. We're not—'

'Yet,' Leo cut in, his voice a husky whisper. 'Consider this a down payment. And tonight you'll think of me, the way I've been thinking of you.' He leaned into her again, nibbled at her lower lip. Teased her mouth into opening for him. Kissed her until the room was spinning.

And then he stopped.

Smiled.

Stroked her face.

'Goodnight, Rose,' he said softly. 'Dream of me tonight. Like I'll dream of you.'

And then he was gone.

CHAPTER SEVEN

LEO held himself in check for the next couple of days. He really needed to be sensible about this. Yes, he wanted Rose. Desired her. But it was temporary. If he concentrated hard enough on his work, he was sure it would pass.

But he just couldn't get her out of his head. And it annoyed him intensely that he had no control over it—the second he let his mind wander, he found himself thinking about her. Remembering how soft her skin had felt beneath his fingertips. How sweet she'd tasted. How much he wanted to pick her up and carry her to his bed and make love with her until neither of them could see straight.

He could ring her. But he'd already called her once. If he called again, it would feel as if he were chasing her. Needy. Weak. He might just as well have the word 'loser' tattooed on his forehead. No, he'd wait a while. If she had the same slow burn he did, the same aching need deep in her gut, she'd call him. And in the meantime he had work to do. A career to keep on the fast track.

No compromises.

'Right.' Sara poured a glass of wine and handed it to Rose. 'Now Daze is asleep and she can't overhear what we're saying, you and I need a little talk.'

'About what?' Rose asked.

Sara cut straight to the point. 'You have to get over Steve.'

'I am over Steve,' Rose protested.

Sara ignored her. 'I know he was a complete and utter bastard, but not all men are like that. There are some good ones around.'

Rose rolled her eyes. 'Yeah, right.'

Sara ruffled Rose's curls. 'See? You've become cynical. What you need is a night out clubbing with me. Pull some totty and have a bit of fun.'

Rose pulled a face. 'Do me a favour. I hated clubbing when I was a teenager. Now it's even worse. I'm too old for clubs. And I don't want to go out on the pull.'

'Anyone listening to you would think you were in your forties! You're only twenty-seven, Rosie. You need to live a little. Let the small stuff wait, once in a while.' Sara rolled her eyes. 'Sometimes I think you're as hopeless a case as my big brother. You need to lighten up. Have fun. You're young, free and single. Enjoy it.' Sara folded her arms. 'And I dare you to accept, the next time someone asks you out.'

Meaning that Sara had someone lined up? Rose groaned. 'I hope you haven't set me up on a blind date or anything. Look, I'm not interested in dating.'

Absolutely true. She didn't want to date Leo. Didn't want to get involved with him. Didn't want to get involved with anyone.

But thinking of Leo, remembering how he'd touched her, made every single nerve-end tingle. She wanted him. She really, really wanted him. There was an aching need in her body that just couldn't be sated by anyone else but Leo.

Maybe she should just break a personal rule and have a one-night stand with him. Get this whole thing out of her system. Though if she rang him and suggested it, he'd think she was cheap. And he already had a low enough opinion of her.

Luckily Sara didn't seem to notice how distracted she was. 'I know, I know, you're not interested in dating. Just in your work.' Sara sighed. 'You know, thanks to Steve the Scumbag, you're in danger of becoming as dried-up as the clothes in your museum.'

'They're not dried up,' Rose protested.

'They are until they've been restored—until they've had some of your TLC. You need a bit of TLC, too,' Sara insisted.

'I'm fine.' Or I would be, if I could get your brother out of my head, Rose thought. But the pictures were there. Worse, she could even feel the heat of his hands, his mouth, against her skin, and it fanned the slow burn of desire until she thought she was going to go crazy.

'Supposing…'

Sara pounced. 'Supposing what?'

'Nothing.'

'Tell me, or I'll nag you until you do.'

Rose knew from experience that her best friend meant it. She sighed. 'I've met someone.'

'I knew it!' Sara crowed. 'About time, too.'

'He's not my type. I'm not his. We're completely wrong for each other.'

Sara's eyes widened in horror. 'Oh, no. Please don't tell me he's another Steve.'

Rose shook her head. She wouldn't be that stupid. Not a second time. Besides, Leo was about as opposite from Steve as it was possible to get. 'He's not a liar or a cheat. And he wouldn't…hurt me.' Not deliberately, anyway.

'So what's the problem? He's married?'

'No.'

'Gay?'

'Definitely not!' The words came out more forcefully than Rose had intended.

Sara lifted an eyebrow. 'If you know that for certain, then something's happened between you.'

Rose felt the colour scorch her cheeks. 'Don't ask for details. You're not getting any.'

'Spoilsport.' Sara grinned. 'If something's happened—even if it's just a kiss—then he's obviously interested.'

Just a kiss? She'd been naked to the waist—and she'd wanted him to go further. Rose squirmed as she remembered just how wanton she'd been in her kitchen. Leo could add a few other things to his list of her undesirable qualities now. Complete lack of restraint being number one.

'If you want him, and he wants you, what's to stop you going for it?' Sara asked.

'I don't want to get involved.'

Sara rolled her eyes. 'You don't have to get *involved* with the guy. Just have some fun. A man to do…' She looked thoughtful for a moment, then smiled. 'Yeah, I reckon it'd do you a lot of good. You know, sex is incredibly good for your skin. It's all to do with orgasms and blood flow.'

This was surreal. Rose couldn't possibly be having this conversation with Sara about her oldest brother. And she'd bet that Sara would say something completely different if she knew that Rose's 'someone' was Leo. Along the lines of never in a million years. 'I don't think I want a man to do,' Rose muttered. Lying through her teeth—because that was exactly what she wanted. With one particular man.

'If you don't want commitment, then that's your only option,' Sara pointed out. 'There isn't anything in between. Either he's a man to do, or he's a man to be serious about.'

That was what worried Rose. She wasn't sure which Leo was. Possibly both.

'Live a little, for once. Have fun.' Sara's eyes sparkled. 'Why don't you ring him? I assume you do have his number?'

'Yes.'

'Then ring him.'

'Maybe.'

'No maybes. Do it. Right now. Give him a call and tell him you want to—oh, pooh. Who's that?' Sara grumbled when her doorbell rang. She put her glass down on the coffee-table and answered the door.

And all the breath went out of Rose's body when she heard Sara's visitor speak. She knew that voice. Gorgeous. Like velvet stroking her skin. It made her want to purr and arch her back. And a hell of a lot more besides.

'So what do *you* want?' Sara demanded.

'Oh, that's a nice way to greet your oldest brother,' Leo said, rolling his eyes. 'And to think I bought you a present.'

'A present with strings?' she asked suspiciously.

'Well, you could offer me a cup of coffee. If that counts as strings.' He removed a box from the bag he was carrying.

'Oh. Chocolate. *Nice* chocolate.' Her eyes glittered. 'I

would invite you in, but Rose is here and you two don't exactly hit it off.'

Had Rose actually said that? Recently? Disappointment balled in his stomach. And there he'd been, hoping that she might call him. What an idiot. Maybe he should leave right now before he made even more of a fool of himself.

But his heart wasn't listening to his head. Yet again. Now he knew that she was here, he wanted to see her. Just see her. Make sure she was OK. It had nothing to do with that trickle of desire running down his spine. 'I'm sure we could manage to be civil to each other. But if it's a problem...' He tucked the chocolates back in the bag, preparing to go.

'No, you don't. They've got my name on them now.' Sara tugged at his arm. 'Give.'

He shrugged. 'As you said, they come with strings.'

'All right, all right, I'll make you a coffee. But don't start being sarcastic or bossy.'

'Bossy?' he deadpanned. 'Not a family trait you've picked up, then.'

Sara gave him a speaking look, but let him in and ushered him through to the living room.

'Rose.' He nodded acknowledgement to her and sat down on the chair furthest from her.

Lord, he'd forgotten just how lovely she was. Those hyacinth-blue eyes. And her lush mouth—he itched to touch. To taste. To carry her to his bed and make her his.

'Leo.'

Her voice was cool, but her eyes betrayed her. She wasn't feeling cool and calm at all. She was decidedly hot and bothered. So whatever she'd said to Sara about not getting on with him...he'd bet it wasn't that recent, then. Certainly not since the night he'd started to make love with her on her kitchen worktop.

She was thinking of that, too. He was sure of it, by the way her hand trembled slightly as it picked up her wineglass.

Sara leaned in from the kitchen doorway. 'Do you really want coffee, Leo? You can have a glass of wine, if you like.'

He smiled at her. 'Thanks, but I'm driving.'

She sighed. 'I know, I know. You never drink even one glass if you're driving.'

'It's not worth the risk. And when you've seen the gory details of as many court cases as I have…'

'Message received, decoded and understood,' Sara said. She came to sit on the arm of his chair. 'So are you going to hand those chocolates over, or not?'

'OK.' He gave her the bag. 'There's something for Daisy in there as well.'

Sara delved into the bag. 'Pens—washable, too. Thanks, she'll love them.'

'Strings attached,' Leo said. 'I want a picture for my office.'

Sara smiled. 'Yeah, OK. Oh, and this too? Leo, you're spoiling her.'

He shrugged. 'Uncle's privilege.'

'Hmm.' She took out a colouring book. 'Stained glass?'

'Translucent pages. When she's coloured them in, if she sticks them on her window it'll look like stained glass,' Leo explained. 'Like the windows a fairy princess would have in her castle.'

Rose was entranced. Leo had been thoughtful enough to buy his niece a present she'd really enjoy. And it hadn't been bought to impress Rose, either—he couldn't have known she'd be here tonight, so he'd been thinking solely of Daisy. And he'd asked for one of Daisy's pictures for his office; clearly he wanted his family near him in his professional environment, too.

Ah, hell. How was she meant to resist a man who cared that much?

And despite the bickering between Leo and Sara, Rose could tell that he really cared about his kid sister. He'd just dropped by to see how she was and leave a present for his niece, and he hadn't forgotten something for his sister either.

Funny, he no longer looked untouchable in his business suit. Though that was probably because he'd touched her—intimately—last time she'd seen him wearing one.

'Thanks.' Awkwardly, Sara gave Leo a hug.

'Big brothers have their uses, sometimes.' He ruffled her hair. 'You promised me coffee. It's rude to keep your guests waiting.'

'You're not a guest,' Sara retorted. 'You could always make it yourself.'

'While you inhale those chocolates? I think not. And you're meant to share—isn't that right, Rose?'

Oh, Lord. She knew he was talking about the chocolates, but it felt as if he were referring to something else entirely.

Something involving sex.

Hot, wild, wanton sex.

Hell. She really had to get a grip.

She mumbled a reply and hoped it would be adequate. Hoped Leo didn't have any idea of just how much he knocked her sideways. Watching him pick out his favourite chocolates was torture, too—he picked out the dark ones. And she could think of something even richer and darker and sweeter than that chocolate. The way his mouth felt over hers, for one.

She drank her glass of wine far too quickly, but it wasn't the alcohol that made her head swim. It was Leo. Being in the same room as him but not being able to touch. Not being able to do what she really wanted to do.

So before Sara could give her a refill, Rose pantomimed a massive yawn. 'Busy week. I'm going to head for home, Sara. Nice to see you, Leo,' she added politely.

Any second now she could escape.

Any second.

'Hang on. Leo can give you a lift home—can't you, Leo?' Sara asked.

Being in a confined space with Leo was more than Rose thought she could handle. 'No, I'll be fine. I'll walk.'

'No way. Not on your own in the evening,' Sara said.

Rose gave a tiny shake of her head. She didn't want Leo asking just why a perfectly fit and healthy woman would be worried about walking through the streets on her own. It wasn't even dark: just the beginning of dusk. There was no reason why she should be afraid.

Apart from what had happened with Steve. The reason why

she still looked over her shoulder before going into her flat. Making sure she hadn't been followed. The same reason she'd taken a martial arts class, with Sara's encouragement: next time—if there ever *was* a next time, and she sincerely hoped there wouldn't be—she'd be prepared. Could get herself out of trouble.

'Sara's right. You're not that far out of my way. It won't be a problem to give you a lift,' Leo said.

She had no choice but to accept his offer. She gave Sara a hug goodbye, then followed Leo down to his car. He didn't bother making conversation once he'd opened the passenger door for her; he simply switched on the CD player. She wasn't surprised to hear Beethoven's ninth symphony; she'd guessed that Leo would prefer classical music to pop—and that he'd prefer traditional to modern. Went with the territory.

What did surprise her was that he flicked forward to the fourth moment. And he actually sang the tenor part of the choral bit. In perfect German. Not in a showing-off way, but as if he were any other man just chilling out and singing along to a favourite pop song on the radio in the car. And his voice was gorgeous. If he ever sang one of her favourite Nat King Cole ballads, she'd be a puddle of hormones.

Leo could have been a perfectly competent professional singer, if he'd chosen. He was the kind of man who could have done anything he wanted. Yet he'd followed the family line. Become a barrister. Wanted to be a QC, like his grandfather. Was it his dream he was fulfilling, Rose wondered, or his grandfather's? She knew Leo Ballantyne the elder had died some years ago—just after Leo the younger had graduated—so had it been a deathbed promise?

What a waste. He could have done anything. Yet he was stuck in a rut.

Maybe she should shake him out of it. Teach him to follow his own dreams.

She was just starting to work out how when he parked on her street. 'I'll see you up.'

'No need.'

'There's every need,' Leo corrected.

She'd opened her door and climbed out by the time he came round to her side of the car; she waited for him to lock the door, then headed for her second-floor flat.

The first time, he'd carried her boxes. She'd invited him in for coffee. He'd kissed her. The second time, he'd just dropped by. She'd ended up naked to the waist. The third time…

Her pulse quickened. The third time, who knew? But all she could think of was Sara's words. A man to do.

A man to do…

Oh, this was bad. She really had to get sex off her brain. But with Leo so close to her—within touching distance—she couldn't think of anything else. Just how good it had felt when he'd touched her. And how good it would be when he touched her properly. And how much she wanted to feel him inside her.

Leo really, honestly, only meant to see Rose to her door. But then she turned to him in her open doorway and smiled. And he was lost. Completely lost. She made him feel completely at sea. No compass. No bearings. He barely knew where he was or what he was doing. Only that his mouth was jammed over hers and he could taste the sweetness of the chocolate she'd eaten at Sara's, mixed with the sweetness of Rose herself. And she was undoing the buttons of his shirt, splaying her hands across his bare chest.

When he broke the kiss, he realised that somehow they'd got through the front door and closed it behind them. One relief, at least—they hadn't started undressing each other in public.

Though it had been very, very close.

He'd been completely oblivious to their surroundings. The only thing he'd been able to concentrate on was the way she tasted and the feel of her skin. He dragged in a breath. 'That really wasn't supposed to happen.'

'No.' She sounded as dazed as he felt. Punch-drunk. As if they'd gone twenty rounds.

'I can't keep my hands off you.' He glanced down at his open shirt. It looked as if he wasn't the only one with that particular problem. He met her gaze, and she flushed.

'Now you think I'm a tart.'

He shook his head. 'No. I think it's the same for you as it is for me. My head's telling me one thing and my heart...my heart's telling me to pick you up and carry you to your bed and to hell with everything else.'

Her expression went from wariness to yearning in about half a second. And then Leo knew what the answer was.

Yes.

CHAPTER EIGHT

So HE did it. He scooped Rose up in his arms, making sure that she had to slide her arms round his neck and hold on. And then he carried her across the room.

'Which door?'

'Right,' she said.

Leo brushed his mouth over hers, and supported her with one arm as he opened her bedroom door with his free hand.

Oh, yes. Just how he'd imagined her. How he'd wanted her. In an old-fashioned boudoir. A wrought-iron bed with white covers, crimson velvet cushions scattered across them, and voile drapes at the head of the bed.

He laid her down on the bed and drew the curtains. It was still just about light enough to see, but he wanted more. The first time he explored her, he wanted to see every expression on her face. Wanted to see what she liked, what made her wriggle, what made her sigh, what made her eyes go unfocused. What made her fall apart in his arms.

And candlelight would be perfect. Not so harsh that she'd feel on display—for all her bravado, he knew that Rose had a slightly shy streak—but bright enough to give him the visual he needed. There was a wrought-iron candle holder next to her bed. Absolutely perfect.

'Matches?' he asked softly.

She took a box from her bedside drawer without comment, and he lit the tea-light on her bedside cabinet. The little candle holder had stars punched through it, letting the light gleam through.

Stars.

Yeah, they'd both be seeing stars by the end of tonight.

He leaned over and kissed her, enjoying the way her mouth opened against his and her fingers splayed against his bare chest. But she was wearing way, way too many clothes for his liking. He needed to be skin on skin. Close and personal. He shifted so that he was lying on his back and she was lying on top of him. Better. His fingers skated along the soft material of her dress until he found the zip. It hissed down slowly, gently. His turn to splay his fingers against bare skin, exploring the dip of her back.

It still wasn't enough.

And he wasn't done with kissing her, either. It took some finessing, but he managed to remove her dress without ruining it and without her leaving his arms. He let the garment fall over the side of the bed—she definitely wasn't going to be needing it any more this evening—and stroked the soft, soft skin he'd uncovered.

Heaven.

She was wearing another black, lacy bra with matching knickers, he noticed. And lace-topped stockings. Every man's dream.

His dream.

Then he felt her muscles tense.

He shifted slightly so he could see her face properly. 'What's wrong?'

'I'm practically naked—and you're fully clothed.'

She was feeling self-conscious? But there was no need. Didn't she know how lovely she was, how desirable he found her? He kissed the tip of her nose. 'And that's a problem?'

'Yes.'

He recognised the flicker of desire in her eyes. The same craving that was running unchecked through his own body. He smiled. 'So what do you suggest we do about it?'

That playful, teasing smile showed Rose a new side of Leo. One she wanted to see more of. And her reaction could bring him closer—or it could drive him away.

She took the risk. 'You could strip.'

'Strip,' he repeated, very softly. For a moment, she thought she'd read the situation completely wrongly. That he was going to recoil.

And then he rolled her gently over to her back, climbed off the bed and stood in front of her. Loosened his tie. Pure silk—she could tell by the way the fabric caught the light. He undid the knot; as she watched his fingers working she knew exactly how they'd be on her body. Skilful. Precise. Deft.

And she could hardly wait.

He hung the tie neatly over her cheval-mirror, then finished what she'd started earlier and unbuttoned his shirt, revealing a muscular chest with a light sprinkling of hair. He'd put any fifties film star to shame, she thought. Leo Ballantyne was simply gorgeous. And with his shirt undone, that little bit dishevelled, he looked incredibly hot.

And he was all hers.

For tonight.

'Keep going,' she directed.

He gave her another of those slow, sensual smiles, and hung his shirt over the mirror. His back view was as good as the front: lean, muscular without being overdeveloped. A perfect triangle of broad shoulders and narrow waist. Smooth skin. The occasional mole, just to make things interesting: she wanted to touch the tip of her tongue to each one. See if the texture and taste of his skin was different there.

And then he turned round and his hands went to the waistband of his trousers.

She couldn't look away. She watched him as he slowly, slowly undid the button and the zip. Eased the soft silk-and-wool fabric down over his thighs.

Lord, he had beautiful legs. Strong. Well-shaped. This was a man she'd like to dress. He'd look fabulous in a full Regency buck's outfit. Or as an eighteenth-century judge, with a red coat and a long curled wig and tight breeches and soft leather boots to the knee.

Or here, in her bedroom, right now, wearing only a pair of boxer shorts. Clingy, soft jersey that hid absolutely nothing.

He'd just stripped. For her.

And she knew it was the cliché to end all clichés, but she couldn't help herself. She licked her lips.

It took him a nanosecond to join her on the bed again. And then he was kissing her, his mouth hot and demanding. Rose gave—and demanded just as much in return. She wanted him. Here. *Now*. She'd never felt anything this urgent before, and it shocked her—but she couldn't do the sensible thing and call a halt to it. She wanted him too badly. So badly, it was like a physical pain. She was going to implode with need.

He was lying flat on her bed underneath her, and this time the barriers between them were much thinner. Only the lace of her bra, acting as an exquisite friction on her hardening nipples. His hands were smoothing down her back, stroking over her bottom, and she could feel the heat and hardness of his erection pressing against her through the soft cotton jersey of his jockey shorts. She could feel his heart beating, strong and fast; clearly he wanted her as much as she wanted him.

But it had been a while, for her. Since Steve. Even though she knew Leo was nothing like Steve—that Leo had more integrity in his little fingernail than Steve had in his entire body—the feeling still unsettled her. She was trusting a man with herself. Supposing she got it wrong, as she had with Steve?

Almost as if he'd sensed that her head had taken over from her heart, Leo sat up, gently moving her with him so that she was kneeling astride him and they were face to face. A corner of his mouth lifted, and he rubbed his thumb along her lower lip. 'You're all tensed up. What's wrong?'

'I…' Oh, Lord. How did she explain this?

But he didn't press her. He just stroked her cheek. 'This thing between you and me—it's not going to go away, you know. We can stop now, but we'll both feel bad. Wondering what we're missing. And it will drive us crazy until we find out.'

She knew he was right. She needed to know. Needed to know how it would feel to have him sheathed inside her. Sooner, rather than later.

'I'm not promising you a relationship—I'm not in a position to have a relationship, right now. I'm not going to lie to you, Rose.'

Not as Steve had. She could believe every word Leo said to her.

'And you don't have to worry. I'm planning to be responsible. I have a condom in my wallet.'

She felt the colour scorch her cheeks. He'd just said he didn't do relationships. How come he was carrying a condom? Or did he think she was that cheap, that easy? Dismay made the words burst out of her. 'So you thought I'd just go to bed with you when you clicked your fingers?'

He stroked her hair away from her forehead. 'More like, all you had to do was whistle and I'd be sitting up begging. Just so you know, I don't make a habit of this. I don't do one-night stands, and I don't let anyone distract me from my goals. But you...' He dipped his head and nibbled her shoulder. 'It was never an *if* something was going to happen between us, it was a *when*,' he murmured against her skin, his breath tickling her. 'And I want you so much, it actually hurts.'

Snap, Rose thought.

The nibbling reached the sensitive cord at the side of her neck, and she arched backwards, closing her eyes. Wanting him to continue. Go south. Ease the ache in her breasts, kiss down over her stomach and, oh, please, a long, slow stroke of his tongue over her clitoris, right where she needed it most.

More nuzzling, this time down her throat to the hollows of her collar-bone. Making her want more and more—and not delivering. Taking it way, way too slowly. Her self-control was in shreds and she was at the point where she was going to beg. Beg him to stop stoking the heat. Beg him to take her right now.

He dropped a kiss in the vee between her breasts, the light contact making her burn.

'Leo, you're driving me crazy,' she whispered.

'I'm with you all the way, honey. Believe me.' He looked her straight in the eye. His pupils were huge and dark, rimmed with an iris the colour of a stormcloud. 'I want to kiss you—all over. Slowly. Every inch. And then do it all over again, until you're burning as much as I am. And then...' He let the promise hang in the air. Tempting her. Giving her the choice.

Her pride shattered. 'Do it,' she whispered. 'Please.' She could hardly get the words out. 'Do it.'

Slowly, he unclasped her bra. Let it drop to the floor. Cupped his hands round her breasts, rubbing his thumbs against her hardened nipples. He dipped his head and took one nipple into his mouth. Sucked until her hands fisted in his hair and she was gasping and rocking her hips against him, way past the point of coherent speech and needing him inside her so desperately, she was going to die.

He kissed his way back up her throat and whispered in her ear, 'The when is now. I'm going to make you see stars, Rose.'

'Oh-h-h.' It came out as a needy little whisper.

He slid one finger underneath her stocking-top, and she quivered. Oh, please, please, let his fingers move. Just a couple of inches north. She tilted her hips in invitation, and he smiled. 'Yes?'

'Yes.' A hiss of pure desire.

Keeping his gaze fixed on hers, he unclipped her suspender and rolled one stocking all the way down her leg. Slowly. Licked the hollow below her anklebone. Tracked up to the spot behind her knee. Oh, since when had *that* been an erogenous zone? But Leo had her shivering. Trembling. Needing more. Oh, please. He was taking it so slowly, she was going to spontaneously combust. She wriggled her hips, urging him with her body to hurry up.

'Mmm. Beautiful.' He worked his way up her inner thigh until she was almost hyperventilating, needing to feel his mouth against her sweet spot. Expecting it. Waiting for that first slow stroke of his tongue.

But then he worked on her other stocking. In reverse. Moving down and down and down. His breath drifting over her thigh. The back of her knee. Her calf. Her anklebone. She could have screamed.

He stopped, and gently finished removing the stocking. Dropped them both on the floor on the other side of the bed. A deft movement by his fingers, and her suspender belt went the same way.

Which left her in a pair of lacy knickers and him in a pair of boxer shorts.

Even. Equal. Matched.

'Tell me,' he invited, his voice a husky whisper.

'I want you.' A shiver ran through her.

'Tell me.' His hands skated across her abdomen and his fingertips traced the edge of her knickers. So near, so far. She couldn't stand this. Her sex was heated, throbbing. She needed him to touch her. Much, much more intimately.

'I want you.' She closed her eyes. 'Inside.' She could hardly get the words out. 'Me.' She dragged in a breath. 'Now. Oh, *now*, Leo.'

When he didn't move or say anything, she opened her eyes in panic.

And then he smiled. 'Better. I want you to see me, Rose. I want to see you. I want to see everything you're feeling in those beautiful hyacinth eyes.' His hands spanned either side of her waist, his fingers gently urging her to lift her bottom. And then he peeled her lace knickers down, achingly slowly.

She felt the colour scorch into her cheeks as he looked at her. She was naked, completely exposed to him. No secrets. No barriers.

'You're so lovely, you make me ache. You take my breath away,' he said, his voice soft.

It was her turn to have her breath taken away when he stood up, took the condom from his wallet, and then peeled off his boxer shorts in one lithe movement.

And then he joined her on the bed and Rose stopped thinking. Like him, she explored with her hands and her mouth. Found out for herself how hard his muscles were, how soft his skin was. How the hairs on his chest tickled her skin. How strong his thighs were. How perfect his gluteal muscles were.

She also learned how and where he liked being touched. How she could make his breath hiss with pleasure. How she could draw soft little moans from him. And, little by little, she grew braver. Explored more. Stroked him and nuzzled him and teased him with her tongue until he was quivering with need.

'Now?' he asked hoarsely, nuzzling her earlobe.

'Now.'

But when he ripped open the foil packet, she closed her fingers over his.

He shuddered. 'You pick one hell of a time to change your mind, Rose!' He closed his eyes. 'OK. I'm not going to force you to do something you don't want to do. Give me a couple of minutes to cool down.'

He respected her that much?

Talk about melting her heart. The more so because he was absolutely genuine. He really meant it. Although he was at a white-heat pitch of desire, he'd stop if she wanted to. He'd put her needs first.

Something Steve had never done.

'I'm not changing my mind. And I'm ready.' So ready. So hot and wet and ready for him that she was going to implode, any second. 'It's just…I think this is *my* job.' She took the condom from him, and he exhaled sharply as she rolled it over his erect penis.

'Oh, yes,' he breathed. 'Touch me, Rose. And I need to touch you. Taste you. I need you.'

And then she was flat on her back, with Leo nudging between her thighs.

'Now,' she said softly, sinking back into the pillows and closing her eyes.

When he didn't move, she opened her eyes again looked up. 'What's wrong?'

'I told you, I want to see your eyes,' Leo said quietly. 'The first time I enter you, I want you to know it's *me* inside you.'

Oh, yes. She knew, all right.

Rose almost came when he slid inside her, his gaze locked on hers. She'd never felt so naked, so open—she knew he could see everything in her eyes. Every jolt of pleasure as he eased into her. Just as she could see his eyes widening with pleasure, desire burning in his face.

She reached up, pulled his head down to hers, and jammed her mouth over his as he began to move. Filling her completely.

Sex with Steve had been good, but it was nothing compared to this. Leo was intense, concentrated. Passionate with a capital P. This was a man who'd take her to her limits, and then beyond.

His hands slid up her thighs, urging her to wrap her legs round him and tilt her hips slightly. She did so, and her breath hitched as he slid deeper still. 'Oh, God, yes,' she hissed against his mouth. 'More.'

She asked; he gave. Everything.

He'd promised her stars.

And that was exactly what she saw as she climaxed.

Afterwards, Rose lay curled in Leo's arms. They didn't need to speak; just being close was enough. She could feel the beat of his heart under her cheek, strong and steady—comforting and yet alarming at the same time.

They'd just made love. Been as intimate as you could get. So would Leo expect to stay for the whole night?

And when was the last time she'd spent the whole night with a man anyway?

Steve.

Who'd let her down.

Who'd lied to her and hurt her and left her life in ruins.

Panic rippled through her. 'It's getting late,' she said.

Leo teased one nipple into hardness. 'Is this your way of telling me to go home?'

Uh. She had to ignore the fact that he was distracting her. Especially as he was doing it so well. 'I have to work tomorrow.'

'Me, too.'

He worked on a Saturday? But he hadn't, last week. Or maybe that had just been because he was worried about Daisy.

The question must have shown in her face because he explained, 'I'm in the middle of a big case. I need to put the hours in.'

'So you need your sleep.'

'Not as much as the average person.'

That figured. Because there was nothing average about Leo Ballantyne.

He gave her a lazy, sensual smile. ' 'I was planning to let you have *some* sleep tonight. Probably not a great deal, I admit—but some.'

She wasn't ready for him to stay. Wasn't ready to share her space. 'Leo. I... This isn't a relationship.'

'Understood. Absolutely.' He paused for just long enough to make her nervous, then added, 'And it isn't a one-night stand, either.'

'So what the hell is it, then?'

He teased her other nipple. 'We could just let it happen and find out. Keep it between us.'

'So now I'm your dirty little secret?'

'No.' He stole a swift kiss. 'It's just nothing to do with anyone else.'

It felt like being a secret to her. Then again, she'd been the first one to say it wasn't a relationship, so how could she complain?

At her silence, he sighed. 'Rose, I can't promise you for ever. I told you that right at the start, and nothing's changed. But I don't want this to stop, either.'

Right now, with his fingers drifting over her hip, she didn't want it to stop, either. But she had to be sensible. She wasn't going to let herself get involved. Wasn't going to get her heart broken. 'I…' Hell. How could she put it into words?

He brushed his mouth against hers again. 'You want me to go.'

'Yes. No. Yes.'

He smiled wryly. 'Me, too. Caught between our heads and our hearts. But you're working tomorrow. I'd better let you get some rest.' He climbed out of bed; when she was about to join him, he shook his head. 'Stay put. You look cute. Like a little dormouse.' When she pulled a face, he laughed. 'Did you know dormice have blue eyes?'

'How do you know all these facts?' she asked.

'It's a male thing. Trivia.'

She chuckled. 'And I bet you're competitive with it.'

'*Moi?* As if,' he deadpanned. 'Did you know, during your lifetime, you'll accidentally eat eight spiders?'

'Oh, that is gross!' And she'd never have guessed that Leo had a teasing streak. That he had such an appealing mischievous-little-boy grin.

She'd also never have guessed how much she enjoyed watching Leo dress. Stripping in reverse. Covering up all the places she'd kissed, stroked, touched. She might be his secret—but he was also hers.

When he'd finished dressing, he leaned down again and kissed her lightly. Just once.

'Sweet dreams.'

They'd be sweet, all right, Rose thought as she snuggled back under the duvet. Because they'd be of Leo, the way he made her feel.

And she couldn't remember the last time she'd felt this good. If ever.

CHAPTER NINE

ONCE wasn't enough, Leo thought, drumming his fingers on the edge of his desk. Last night had been meant to—well—get it out of their systems. But it hadn't worked. Not for him.

Ah, hell. Everything about this was plain wrong. He was letting Rose distract him from his work—from his goal plans. He'd been at his desk for three hours and he'd done virtually nothing. He hated wasting time. But he'd been sitting here doodling and thinking about how Rose's mouth had felt against his bare skin and how much he liked the jasmine-vanilla scent of her perfume. How it had felt to ease into her body. How her body had tightened around his and sent him tipping over the edge.

Not good. Not good at all.

A cold shower didn't put him back in focus, either. Nor did an extremely strong cup of coffee.

If he called her now, she'd think he was too keen.

If he didn't call her, he'd get absolutely nothing done and waste the rest of the day—probably the rest of the weekend.

Pride or compromise?

It wasn't much of a choice. Cross with himself for letting his heart overrule his head, he called her mobile phone.

'Hello, Rose.'

'Leo.'

She sounded wary as a cat. Not that he could blame her. It was how he felt, himself. So what now? Ask her if she slept well?

Leo hated this. Hated feeling like a gauche teenager wanting to ask a girl for a date and worrying that he'd be turned down.

For goodness' sake, he was thirty-two. Way past all that. It shouldn't matter if she turned him down.

But it did. And it annoyed him. Because it meant he wasn't in control—and Leo Ballantyne was always, always in control.

'Are you busy tonight?' he asked.

'Not sure.'

Meaning yes, she was, but she didn't want to sound too eager, either? 'If you're free, maybe you'd like to have dinner with me. My place.'

A pause.

He only realised he'd been holding his breath when she answered, 'What time?'

'Pick you up at eight?'

Another pause. 'OK. See you then.'

It wasn't a relationship. Wasn't a one-night stand. Rose had absolutely no idea where this was going. She should have said no. If she'd had any sense at all, she would've said no.

But he'd said dinner. At his place. She already knew he cooked well; after a hard day at work, she didn't always want to mess around in the kitchen; and, besides, she was intrigued to know what Leo's personal space was like. Whether it would be neat and orderly and very precise, or whether it would give her some clue about what made him tick.

Who was she trying to kid? She wanted to see him. Touch him. Dinner wasn't just going to be dinner. She knew exactly what was on offer. And, even though her head was telling her this was a stupid idea, her heart was doing a little victory dance.

At eight o'clock precisely, Leo buzzed her entryphone. She pressed the button. 'On my way down.'

He was waiting just outside; she'd almost forgotten how good-looking he was. Those storm-grey eyes, the mouth that promised passion—passion she'd already experienced with him.

Her man. A pulse beat low in her stomach at the thought.

Then her head stepped in with a reminder. *Temporarily.*

So she greeted him coolly, formally. 'Thank you for inviting me to dinner.'

'Pleasure.' Just as cool and formal. And Leo, as a barrister, was very, very good at being formal.

Though she knew what he looked like when his face was heated with passion. How he breathed when he climaxed. The look in his eyes. What his body felt like inside hers.

Oh-h-h. She really had to stop thinking about that.

'I, um, forgot to ask you if you'd prefer red or white. So I played safe.' She handed him a bottle of pinot grigio.

'Thank you.' He smiled his acceptance, shepherded her to his car, and drove them back to Clerkenwell.

His apartment block was very modern, but the design was good—clean lines, not pretending to be something it wasn't. Strangely, it fitted in with the older buildings around it—almost as if it were comfortable with itself. Rose could understand why Leo had bought a flat here.

And she wasn't in the slightest bit surprised when they ended up at the penthouse. Leo *would* own the best flat in the building.

He let them in, and gave her a whistle-stop tour. 'Kitchen.' Separate, rather than open plan, she noticed—and it looked like a show kitchen. Immaculate, every surface gleaming. Though the whole effect was undermined by what looked like a couple of Daisy's paintings, held onto the door of the fridge by a magnet. Surface gloss and a warm heart.

Like Leo himself, perhaps.

'Bathroom.' Very plain and simple. Functional. Masculine.

He skipped past one door—the one she assumed was his bedroom.

A room she might see later. The thought made her pulse speed up.

'Living room.'

It was stunning. Not the décor—everything was neutral—but the room was huge and overlooked the city. More interestingly, there were two sets of French doors. Why would a penthouse have French doors?

'Balcony,' he said, indicating one. 'Roof terrace.'

'May I?'

'Sure.' He unlocked the doors to the roof terrace. To her

delight and surprise, there were pots of flowers everywhere on the paving slabs. There was a large choisya, with glossy green leaves and hundreds of white flowers over it. Terracotta pots of sweet peas, winding up round an elongated pyramid-shaped structure and scenting the evening air. A yucca in a blue-glazed pot. A terracotta trough containing herbs—she recognised basil, mint, rosemary, and flat-leafed parsley—and, contrary to all her expectations, more blue-glazed pots, this time containing bright orange gerberas.

Nothing like she'd thought he'd have. 'Wow.'

He shrugged. 'There's no point in having a roof terrace if you're not going to use it properly.'

And he clearly used it—apart from the fact that the plants looked well cared for, there was a chair and table smack in the middle of it.

'You sit out here after work?'

'And during,' he admitted. 'In the summer.'

Ah, yes. His computer equipment would be state-of-the-art. Wireless. So he wouldn't need to be indoors, near a socket or a phone line.

'Let me get you a drink. Wine?'

'White would be lovely, thank you.'

Speaking as if they were strangers, so polite to each other. Who'd have thought that they'd ripped each other's clothes off, last night, unable to get enough of each other?

But that had been last night. Now was…different.

'I'll bring it through,' he said, and disappeared.

She pottered around his living room while he was busy in the kitchen. There was nothing to show his personality in the room except for the framed photos on the mantelpiece—one of Daisy on a lawn, holding a flower; one of his parents; one of Sara laughing; and one of Sara with her three brothers, which was clearly a formal family portrait, probably taken to celebrate a birthday or anniversary.

There was a desk in one corner with a state-of-the-art computer. The bookcase nearest the desk held legal texts, as she'd expected, but also housed an eclectic mix of classic literature and historical military fiction. An expensive hi-fi system sat next to it, and a plasma-screen TV.

'Boys and their toys, hmm?' Leo said, returning with two glasses of chilled wine before she'd had a chance to look through his music and film collection.

'You said it.' She accepted hers gratefully and tasted it. Definitely not the wine she'd brought him—this was chilled, for a start. To exactly the right temperature. Chablis, she'd guess. Probably vintage, because Leo was clearly used to the best. But it didn't seem as if he was boasting, showing off just how much money he had. Although his flat was expensive—she couldn't afford something like this in a million years—and the décor was almost like that of a show home, that roof garden clinched it. This was his personal space. His little patch of green in the city. And he'd invited her here tonight. Into his private world. Somewhere she guessed he didn't invite people very often.

Dinner was fabulous. A chilled, summery courgette soup with crispy wholegrain rolls; a Mexican-inspired salad based around avocado, kidney beans, rice and peppers, with a lime and chilli dressing; and tiny Scottish raspberries served with crème brûlée. Rich, dark coffee; and the most exquisite chocolates Rose had ever tasted.

His mouth had tasted of chocolate, last night. When he'd kissed her outside her front door and the world had gone a little fuzzy.

A *lot* fuzzy.

The temperature just felt as if it had gone up ten degrees. Twenty.

'Don't tell me you made the chocolates yourself,' Rose said, trying to wrench her mind off the track of having sex with Leo.

He gave her one of those quirky smiles she liked so much. 'No. Nor the bread. There's an excellent deli within walking distance.'

She noticed immediately what he'd left out. Ninety per cent of the meal. 'You made all the rest of this for me?'

He shrugged. 'I have to eat, too.'

But he wasn't vegetarian. And this meal was. He'd taken a lot of trouble to make it good for her. 'Thank you.'

He inclined his head in acknowledgement.

She wished he hadn't put a candle between them on his

dining table. It reminded her too much of last night. Making love in candlelight.

Which was what she wanted to do right now. She had this insane urge to stand up, walk round to his side of the table, sit on his lap and kiss him stupid.

Instead, she gulped her coffee. And almost choked when it went down the wrong way.

He was at her side in a second, patting her back until she caught her breath. Just as he would have done for any guest...except he was touching her. Bodily contact. From there it was a natural step to sliding her arms round him, too. Tipping her face up as his mouth descended on hers.

He kissed her. Soft and sweet. Little nuzzling, exploring kisses that made her open her mouth to him, let him deepen the kiss.

Time stopped. Everything stopped except her awareness of this man, the way he made her feel. The strong, steady beat of his heart under her palm.

Kiss him stupid? More like the other way round.

She had to get a grip. Get control of herself. And she would, if he'd stop kiss—

Oh-h-h. She sank back against soft, soft pillows.

Leo's bed.

They were in Leo's bedroom.

'How'd we get here?' she asked. She couldn't even remember leaving his living room. Couldn't remember anything except kissing him. His mouth trailing over her collar-bones, his fingers teasing the skin at the edge of her dress's neckline.

'Walked. I think.' He sounded as dazed as she felt.

'This isn't supposed to happen. We're not having a relationship.' She'd been self-sufficient ever since Steve. She hadn't needed anyone to make her feel more valid as a person. She'd been perfectly happy with her life. She didn't want a relationship.

He laughed softly. 'I don't want this either, but right now I think it's out of our control.'

Our control, she noted. So he was knocked sideways, too.

But his hands were sliding down her sides, moulding her curves, and her words of protest faded before she could even speak them. 'Yes,' she said, meaning it. Wanting him. Needing him.

The next few seconds were a blur. But then she was aware of cool, very smooth and very soft sheets against her naked back, and Leo's hot, hard body pressed against her front.

Skin to skin.

So close, but not close enough. She wanted the ultimate closeness. Now, now, now. She wanted to feel as good as he'd made her feel last night. She wanted the thrill of knowing that this proud, clever, capable man could lose control when he was in her arms.

And then at last his body eased into hers. Filling her. Lord, it felt good. So good. With every thrust, he took her closer and closer to the edge. As she climaxed she gasped out his name, heard his answering cry and felt his body shudder.

Leo shifted to lie on his back, curving his arm round her so her head was pillowed on his chest. She draped her arm across his washboard-flat stomach, cuddling into him. Funny how just lying here quietly with him made her feel good. Safe and warm. Protected.

But this wasn't where she belonged. Leo's lifestyle wasn't hers. His world would never accept her. They really ought to stop this now, while it would still be easy.

Except she had a nasty feeling it was already too late.

CHAPTER TEN

A MONTH. He'd been seeing Rose for a month. And the feelings still weren't out of his system. In fact, Leo was pretty sure they were getting worse. He really couldn't stop thinking about her. She was so different from any other woman he'd ever met: in the way she dressed, the way she thought, the way she acted.

She'd introduced him to new things—torch singers from the fifties, paper dosa in a vegetarian curry house in Whitechapel, and a memorable Thursday when she'd persuaded him to take a day's holiday and go to Birmingham Rag Market with her to get new stock for her stall. He hadn't been keen on the idea of going to what sounded like a glorified jumble sale, but they'd left at the crack of dawn, she'd told him exactly what to look for, and he'd discovered how much fun it was bartering for pieces.

Especially when he'd beaten her to a prize find—a set of Bakelite buttons.

'They could be plastic,' Rose said.

He scoffed. 'I think not. The stallholder said they were Bakelite.'

'*Said*. Was the word "probably" next to it?'

'No. So that's a contravention of the—'

She pressed a finger against his lips. 'You're not a lawyer today. You're a market trader. And you need to do a quick and dirty test on this sort of thing to make sure of what you're buying—before you buy it.'

He nibbled her finger. 'Quick and dirty. Mmm.'

Her cheeks turned scarlet, and he smiled. He loved the way he could make her blush so easily.

'Mind out of gutter,' she said primly. 'Now.'

'Yes, boss. I'm very penitent.'

She gave him a speaking look, then went into lecture mode. Another thing he loved. Rose was passionate about her work, and it showed.

'Bakelite. Watch and learn.' She tapped one of the buttons. 'OK, it sounds heavy. That's a good sign.' She tested its weight in her hand. 'Mmm, heavier and denser, too, than I'd expect plastic to be. You might be right.'

'I am,' Leo insisted.

'Friction test.'

'Friction.' That word raised all sorts of interesting possibilities. She knew it, too, because she coloured again. Knowing exactly what kind of friction he meant. The friction between their bodies.

'Leo. I'm trying to teach you something.' She rubbed the button against the hem of her dress, then sniffed it. 'Yep. Smell.'

He did, and grimaced. 'What is that?'

'Carbolic acid. Bakelite smells like that when it gets hot, though plastic doesn't. OK.' She smiled at him. 'You win the prize for best find of the day.'

He nuzzled the curve of her neck and whispered in her ear, 'Which is?'

She stole a kiss. 'Not something I can give you in the middle of a public place. Well, not unless you want to end up in court on an indecency charge,' she added with a grin.

'We'll take a rain check. Until we're back in Camden.'

He'd nearly ended up with a speeding fine in his hurry to get back to London, and she'd made love to him with an intensity that had made him want to cheer and cry at the same time.

And now he realised something that made his heart sink. For the first time since he was a teenager, he was in a situation where he just wasn't in control. He was falling in love—correction, *had* fallen in love. With practically the most unsuitable woman in the world. Like his godmother Natasha, Rose wouldn't fit into his world as a barrister's partner—and if he made their relationship public, he would be putting everything he had worked for so incredibly hard for at risk.

It was going to come to the point where he had to make a choice. His career or Rose. Except he knew he'd be miserable without either of them. Deeply, deeply miserable. He loved his job. He loved being able to make a real difference to people's lives. He loved the fact that he was carrying on a family tradition and flying the flag for his generation.

But he also loved Rose. He loved her vibrancy and her passion and her independence and the way she made him feel. OK, so she wasn't the flaky airhead he'd first believed her to be, but he knew she wasn't going to fit into the traditionalist, almost old-fashioned world he moved in.

Hell, hell, hell. His life was sliding apart, and somehow he had to get the pieces to fit back together. Heart and head, head and heart. They had to go in the same direction again. But how?

Later that evening, Rose was curled up with Leo in bed. 'Want to tell me about it?' she asked.

'About what?'

'Why you've been brooding all evening?'

'I'm not brooding.'

She scoffed. 'Leo, you've hardly said a word to me tonight. Is it work?'

He shook his head. 'Leave it.'

'Nothing to bother my pretty little head about?' she asked.

Clearly he heard the edge in her voice because he sat up. 'Since when have I ever patronised you?'

She raised an eyebrow. She could think of a few times in the past. In the days when he'd barely acknowledged her existence.

He obviously knew it, too, because he looked faintly guilty. 'Not since we've been—'

'Not seeing each other,' Rose supplied wryly. They'd both agreed that what was happening between them wasn't a relationship with a future. Neither of them had mentioned the L-word. This was just a mixture of—well—of an unlikely friendship and sex. Not permanent. Not a one-night stand.

Something they didn't talk about, but was happening all the same.

She reached up to stroke his face. 'OK. I take it back. So what's wrong?'

He sighed. 'Nothing. Why didn't you tell me about your museum work?'

She blinked. 'That's a bit out of left field.'

'And you're evading the question.'

'I'm not in the dock. I don't have to explain myself to you.'

'I know.' He slid back down the bed and gathered her into his arms. 'I just wondered, that's all. I mean, Daisy showed me your display at the museum. I read your leaflet. Clearly you love your work and you've got a gift for explaining to people—I was fascinated by your piece about the life of a tailor in Victorian London. Starting at age twelve, doing menial jobs for two years and then working through five years of apprenticeship. And, even worse, the seamstresses—working from six in the morning until midnight to make three shirts a day.'

'For two and a half old pence each. And they had to buy their thread out of that,' Rose said. 'The conditions were appalling. Seven buttonholes per shirt—and if they didn't do it right, they'd get nothing. They'd literally work their fingers to the bone.'

He nodded. 'And the people who bought the clothes or wore them wouldn't think about the sweatshop conditions of the way the clothes were produced.'

Leo clearly understood that. Which wasn't what she'd expected, considering what he did for a living. It must have shown on her face, because he asked, 'What are you thinking?'

'Just that—well, in my experience, prosecutors wouldn't worry about that sort of thing.'

He laughed. 'You'd be surprised. Actually, I don't always prosecute. I can work for either side of a case.'

Mmm, and that was something that worried her. 'Could you work for someone if you thought they were in the wrong?'

He looked thoughtful. 'Intellectually, it would be a challenge—but, no, I wouldn't take the case. It'd be morally bankrupt.'

Only then did she realise she'd tensed up, when relief flooded through her. She hadn't read him wrong. Leo would always do what was right.

'And I hate these professional victims,' Leo continued. 'Negligence law should be there to protect people, not used as a way to get rich quick. That way everyone loses, and I think the duty of care works both ways. You have a responsibility to look after yourself as well as to be looked after.'

Responsibility. She knew how big he was on responsibilities. 'So you don't always side against Goliath?'

'Not if Goliath's in the right. If someone sued a school, say, because she slipped on ice while she was carrying a baby.'

Rose frowned. 'But the school should've made sure the paths were safe.'

'Put it this way, if you were taking Daisy to nursery when she was a babe in arms, and you were late, and it was snowy and icy underfoot, would you run or would you walk?'

'Walk, of course,' Rose said. 'It isn't safe to run on ice. And I think I'd use a buggy—then, if I slipped, I wouldn't drop the baby or fall on her.'

'Exactly. In this case, the woman had a record of bringing her child to school late. She slipped because she was running—and the school had cleared proper pathways in the snow. Because she wasn't paying attention to where she was going, she strayed off the path and slipped. The baby was OK, I should add—she was trying to claim for a back injury. And, even after the incident, the woman was still late for school most days and ended up running through the playground.'

'Maybe she had another child to drop off first.'

Leo rolled his eyes. 'Which is one of the reasons why people share the school run. To avoid time clashes. But, actually, she didn't. She just wasn't good at planning her time, and she wanted to blame someone else for her own guilt at nearly hurting her baby.' He smiled. 'Are you sure you aren't a lawyer in disguise?'

'Nearly was.'

The words slipped out before she could stop them.

Leo went very, very still. 'How do you mean, you nearly were? Was law the course you applied for before you went to art college?'

Damn, the man was sharp. Had a good memory. She hadn't told him very much about it at all—and it had been ages ago.

'Yes. For a couple of terms. It…' She paused. She hated remembering all that unhappiness. The way she'd tried so hard to follow her father's dream and join the family practice. Except she'd hated it. She'd so nearly gone under. And if she told Leo about her nervous breakdown, maybe he'd think she was weak. Feeble. She didn't want that. 'It just wasn't me,' she said finally.

'The law doesn't suit everyone.' He held her closer. 'Are your parents lawyers?'

'Dad and my eldest brother are. My mum and my middle brother are accountants.'

'And you felt you ought to follow in their footsteps?'

She nodded.

'There's nothing wrong with that.'

'Isn't there?' In her view, there was a lot wrong. And that was part of the problem with Leo. She shifted to prop herself up on one elbow and looked at him. 'You can't live someone else's dreams, Leo. It's not healthy. Look at you—you're driving yourself at a ridiculously hard pace to copy your grandfather's record of being one of the youngest ever QCs. And why? Because of some promise you made to him when you were still a kid, too young to know what it meant?' And Leo, with his strong sense of responsibility, would believe that he had to follow through. Keep his promise regardless.

'That's not the issue.'

'Yes, it is. You're doing what your whole family expected you to do—being a barrister. Didn't you ever want to be a history teacher or a captain of a ship or a racing-car driver?'

His jaw was set. 'No. I wanted to be a lawyer, and I'm a good one.'

'You'd have been good at anything you wanted to do.' Rose shook her head in exasperation. Didn't he realise that he was one of these people who could excel at whatever he turned his hand to? 'Your singing voice is gorgeous. You'd be a pin-up in dozens of countries if you'd become a singer.'

'I didn't want to be a singer or an international pin-up. I wanted to be a lawyer.'

'Did you? Or is it something that was said to you right from when you were in your pram? Little Leo, named after his grandfather, spitting image of the old man, bound to be a chip off the old block, of course he's going to be a lawyer and break the same records?'

'I think,' Leo said carefully, 'it's time for me to go home. Before I say something we both regret.'

He dressed swiftly and in silence. And he didn't kiss her goodbye when he left. Rose did nothing to stop him, angry that he wouldn't even discuss it properly with her and he'd dismissed her views as meaningless.

Though when the door closed behind him, she drew her knees up to her chin and wrapped her arms round them. Maybe she'd just solved the problem of having Leo Ballantyne in her life.

Or maybe she'd just made the biggest mistake of her life.

Right at that moment, she wasn't sure which.

The following morning, Rose's eyes felt heavy and her head was throbbing. She managed to set up her stall as usual, but somehow the usual spark was missing. She didn't feel like chatting to her customers, the way she usually did, helping them to find something that would suit their colouring and shape and make them feel good. She didn't find her usual delight in the colours and textures of the clothes on her stall.

And she knew why.

Because she felt guilty about Leo. She'd pushed him too far. Worse, she'd hurt him.

Mid-morning, she asked Janey to look after her stall. Found herself a quiet corner. And rang him.

He answered at the second ring. 'Ballantyne.'

Abrupt. Well, he was probably working at his desk and had answered the phone out of force of habit. 'Leo, it's Rose.'

'Oh.' His voice grew noticeably cooler.

'I owe you an apology. For last night.'

Silence.

'I'm sorry.'

'Uh-huh.'

She sighed. 'You're not going to make this easy for me, are you?'

'I don't like being treated as if I'm weak-minded,' Leo said. 'As if I'm not capable of making my own choices.'

She dragged in a breath. 'That's not what I said.'

'No? How did it go? I only became a barrister because it was something that was said to me right from when I was in my pram?' He definitely didn't sound pleased. 'Conditioning. Like Pavlov's dogs.'

'What I meant was,' she said softly, 'you're the sort who'd honour every promise you made. Put your family's needs first. You'd sacrifice your own dreams if you thought it would make your grandfather happy.'

'He died before I could be called to the Bar.'

'But I bet you raised a glass to him that night. And I bet he knew. And it would've gone against your sense of honour to back out after he died, even if you didn't really want to be a barrister.'

'I did want to be a barrister, Rose. I still do. I happen to like what I do for a living.'

'Skewer people.'

'When they deserve it, yes. Rose, think about it. There are the people who're desperate for a better life, come here in the most appalling and dangerous conditions, work for well below the minimum wage and don't complain because at least by working here they can send something home to help their families—all the while, being preyed on by the people who should be helping them.' He made a noise of self-disgust. 'Ah, don't get me started about that.'

'Is that what you're working on now? Illegal immigration?'

'Yes and no. It's a gangmaster case, but I can't say any more about it than that.'

She didn't need to ask whose side he was fighting on. It was obvious now: Leo fought for the underdog. And he was passionate about the cause. Believed in doing the right thing.

No wonder he'd been so hostile to her, when he'd thought she'd knowingly been trafficking in stolen goods. Because it went against everything he believed in: fairness, truth and justice.

And maybe she'd been unfair to him. Tarred him with the same brush as the lawyers who'd worked on her own case and the type of people she'd met when she'd studied law. Not believing that he could actually want to be a barrister to help people, to follow his own dream as well as that of his family.

He sighed. 'Why are we having this conversation?'

'Because I'm at work and you're at home and—look, I'm sorry. I didn't mean to insult you or hurt your pride.'

'Oh, so now I'm touchy as well?'

'Actually,' Rose said, 'you bloody well are. And for someone who usually has impeccable manners, you're not accepting my apology very gracefully.' Annoyed, she hung up.

Almost immediately, her mobile phone beeped. Text message.

Probably Sara. She glanced at the message screen, then frowned. Leo. Probably a message to tell her to go to hell—he'd hate not having the last word.

She flicked into the message.

Dinner tonight. Menu: humble pie for two.

Just when she wanted to strangle him, he did something that knocked her off balance. Like now. He'd made her laugh. And he was right—they were both being stupid about this.

Rapidly, she texted back: *Don't eat umbles. Am veggie.*

The reply was almost instant. *And you call *me* a smart alec?*

Ah, she'd missed him. The quickness of his responses. She liked his mind, the way he tuned into things instantly.

Who was she kidding? The way she felt about Leo Ballantyne wasn't just liking. But it was something she wasn't really ready to think about. Much too scary.

Another beep from her phone. *Your place. 7.30. I'll bring takeaway.*

Deal. Thanx, she responded.

As usual, he was exactly on time.

'Are you ever spontaneous?' she asked. 'Does it ever occur to you to turn up early? Or late?'

'If you're late,' Leo said, 'it implies the other person's time is worth nothing. Which is rude, inconsiderate and arrogant. If you're early, you'll either end up waiting—which wastes time— or you'll put unfair pressure on someone. Anyway, that's not my definition of spontaneous.'

'What is?'

He smiled. 'I was hoping you'd ask that. Your kitchen usually makes me spontaneous.'

Oh, yes. She remembered that night.

'And I've been having thoughts about my roof garden.'

'Your roof garden?' At his nod, she queried, 'Such as?'

'Ah, now. It wouldn't be spontaneous if I told you beforehand.'

She glowered at him. 'You're splitting hairs.'

He shrugged. 'I'm a lawyer. Goes with the territory. Now, are we going to eat this before it gets cold?'

He'd brought a selection of Thai food; she shared it between two plates while he set her little bistro table. 'Would you have called me if I hadn't called you?' she asked, halfway through the meal.

'I don't know. Maybe.' He sighed. 'Yes. I was miserable last night.'

'Me, too,' she admitted.

'Careful. It's beginning to sound like a relationship.'

His tone was light, but the warning was clear. They were on the verge of stepping into new territory. She heeded the warning and changed the subject quickly. 'So you think people should follow their dreams, then?'

He nodded. 'It's better to do what you love, and do it well, than do something to please someone else and never really reach your potential.'

'So why was your family so hard on Sara about art college?' she asked.

'Because when she first told everyone she wanted to go to art college, we thought she would do what she always did: start something new only to get bored and give it up. And by the time we had all come round to the idea and knew she was doing something she loved, something she had huge potential in, she dropped out.'

'Because she was pregnant.'

'Other people manage to study with kids. Mature students. She could've gone back at least part-time. But she didn't even try. And right now she's not stretching herself to what she really could be. Working part-time on your stall is a compromise. Like all her other temporary part-time jobs. She never sticks at

anything, just drifts along and hopes it'll turn out for the best.
But maybe when Daisy starts school, she might decide to go back
to college.'

She had now. But Rose had promised not to say anything. She
could understand why: Leo clearly shared his family's view that
Sara never stuck at anything. Sara wanted to achieve it by herself,
and then tell them.

'Maybe you should talk to her about it,' Rose said. And she'd
have a quiet word with Sara beforehand, let her know that Leo
wouldn't be unsympathetic: that he realised Sara had an aptitude
for jewellery design and loved doing it, too.

'Maybe.' Leo shrugged. 'Though I'm not suggesting that to
her, because then she'd refuse to go back.'

'Reverse psychology.' Rose digested what he'd just said.
Working on her stall was a compromise. 'So is that what you
think of me, too? That I'm wasting my potential, working on a
market stall?'

'Depends. If you love your museum work, and you're running
the stall as a compromise because you can't get a full-time job
as a curator or a lecturer or a wardrobe adviser for costume
drama—or whatever it is you really want to do—then yes. You're
wasting your passion.'

'Full-time curator jobs are hard to come by.' Especially when
you had the kind of stain on your name that she did.

'And lecturing?'

'Same problem.' Same unspoken problem, too.

'What about a wardrobe department?'

She grimaced. 'I wouldn't have the patience to work with the
prima-donna actor types and I don't want to make replica clothes.
I want to work with the real things. In the museum, I learn things.
I get to work on the most amazing pieces—pieces I'd only see
behind glass otherwise.' He was challenging her now, just the
way she'd challenged him last night. And she could understand
now why he'd got so defensive: she didn't like having to justify
her choices either. 'But I like my stall, too. I get to spend time
with people. I *like* working with people, finding something that
really suits them and brings out their personality.'

'So why a market stall? Why not a shop?'

'Because then I'd have to give up my work at the museum, or I'd have to hire people to cover the shop, or I'd have to get someone else to do the Birmingham run for me—and I like picking my own stock. I don't want to delegate it to someone else. And hiring staff isn't the same as sharing my pitch with other people. I'd have to think about overheads and charging more, and whether it would put off my regular customers now. And I'd miss the buzz of the market. I love the characters among the stall-holders, the atmosphere. The market isn't just some cheap, tacky place, you know.'

'Don't get me wrong. When I say Sara's wasting herself working on a market stall, it's nothing to do with snob values.' Leo's eyes glittered. 'I just believe if you don't have passion for what you do, then you're doing the wrong thing. Life's too short to waste.'

Yeah. She'd second that.

'So let's not waste it,' she said softly. 'Let's not fight any more.'

He opened his arms. 'I think the saying is, "Make love, not war."'

She smiled. 'I thought you'd never ask...'

CHAPTER ELEVEN

A COUPLE of weeks later, Rose was glancing through the local paper on her stall when her eye was caught by a paragraph heading.

LOCAL BUSINESSWOMAN DENIES FRAUD.

She remembered seeing headlines like that before. MARKET TRADER IN FRAUD SCAM. CURATOR ACCUSED OF FENCING STOLEN GOODS.

Headlines that had gone on to name her. Rose Carter.

Of course, they'd been careful to say that she was 'accused,' not that she'd actually done it. So she'd had no recourse afterwards. Not that she'd ever trust a court of law again.

Had this woman been caught the same way? By sheer naivety, a simple desire to help out someone she thought was a friend? The love of her life who'd…

Rose shuddered at the thought and was about to turn the page when a name caught her eye.

Stefan Mahalski.

No. It couldn't be.

She read it more closely, and bile rose in her stomach. Stefan Mahalski, aged twenty-nine. Website designer. Horrified to discover that his fiancée had been laundering stolen computer parts through her shop.

Website designer, hmm? Made a change from being a jewellery designer. But everything else… She'd just bet that he'd suckered this poor woman in the same way he'd suckered Rose. 'I need to help out a friend who's having a bad time, needs to raise some cash quickly. Could you do something?' And she'd been only too willing to do something for her fiancé's friend. Any friend of his was a friend of hers. She took old computers in part-exchange for new systems all the time: of course she'd advance Steve's friend the money. Because, being a friend of Steve, he was perfectly genuine.

Sucker.

And Steve the Scumbag got away with it. Again. He was so convinced he was invincible, he didn't even bother using an assumed name.

God. Why couldn't they look up the court records, see that he'd been the so-called horrified fiancé four years ago? And she'd just bet he'd done the same to other women in other cities. After her case, London would've been too hot for him for a while. So he'd probably moved on to Manchester, Liverpool, Glasgow—another big city where he could disappear at just the right moment. On and on. And now he was back in London and running the same scam on someone else.

Somehow, she had to get in touch with this woman. Warn her to be careful. Tell her what had happened to *her*. Tell her to get a proper credit check run so she could find out just what Steve had done in her name. Tell her to get some kind of protection—because Rose could remember only too well what had happened next.

The mess.

The bruises.

The pain.

The bitter, sick feeling of betrayal. Again and again and again. By someone she'd loved, someone she'd trusted, someone she'd been naïve and stupid enough to believe in.

And then feeling that it was all your fault. That you'd deserved it. The self-loathing. The shame—shame that never entirely went away.

A few phone calls later, she was in no better position. The computer shop said that Lorraine Burrows wasn't currently contactable and refused to pass on a message—and Rose, wondering if any of the assistants might be in league with Steve, wouldn't leave her name or number. The courts weren't helpful and neither was the newspaper. They couldn't release details.

Couldn't pass on a message. And then the newspaper had started asking awkward questions—questions she didn't want to answer. She wanted to help, yes, but she didn't want her past dragged up and spread over the press again.

There was one person who could help.

Leo.

Except that would mean telling him everything. And if he realised just how weak and hopeless she was, he'd despise her. Rose wrapped her arms round herself. She didn't want him to despise her. She didn't want him to walk out of her life. But she couldn't stand by and see the worst bits of her past happen to someone else, either.

Somehow, she had to find a middle course. Get his help without losing his respect. Losing his...love?

Rose was quiet. Too quiet, Leo thought. And she'd barely smiled all evening.

'What's wrong?' he asked.

'Nothing.'

He didn't believe her. Today was her museum day. She normally glowed on Mondays, bubbling about some piece or other she'd been working on. But museums always felt the pinch; had there been cutbacks? Had Rose, as a part-timer, been let go? Or was there a problem at the market, a huge site-fee increase that would hit her stall for six? 'Is it work?' he asked.

She shook her head, but she refused to be drawn.

Leo decided to let it go. Until she was ready to talk. But when they made love, that evening, he felt wetness against his face.

She was crying.

Silently.

He stopped. Held her close. Stroked her hair. 'Talk to me, honey. Tell me what's wrong. Maybe...' This was a risk, but one he had to take. Either it would push her into a declaration of independence, or she'd realise that it was OK to lean on him. 'Maybe I can help you fix whatever the problem is,' he said softly. He wasn't going to take over; he wanted to do it as a team. Please, let her realise that. He'd never, ever take away her independence. He'd begun to realise how important it was to her.

She shuddered. 'I…need to get dressed. So do you.'

'Why?'

'I need a shower. I feel unclean.'

He stared at her in shock. Unclean? 'Because of me?'

Her breath hitched. 'No. Not you. It's… I need some space.'

Space? He didn't like the sound of this. Was this the beginning of the end?

But he did what she clearly wanted and moved away.

'Just let me shower and get dressed. I can do this easier if I'm dressed.'

Why did she feel unclean? And what would be easier if she dressed? He didn't understand. Though he could see that if he pushed her now, she'd crack. She needed careful handling. Although he wanted to roar with frustration and demand that she told him what the hell was going on in her head, he forced himself to be gentle. 'You know where the fresh towels are. Help yourself to what you need. I'll make us a drink, yes?'

'Thank you.'

She was shivering. With fear? He couldn't bear it. Couldn't bear that she was hurting and she wouldn't let him close enough to make it all right. 'Rose.' He reached over and hugged her, just once. 'It's going to be OK. Whatever it is, I promise it's going to be OK.' He'd make it all right for her. He'd move mountains for her. He just hoped she understood that.

While she was showering, he dressed quickly and made her a mug of hot chocolate and himself a double espresso. Sat on the sofa and waited for her.

When she walked into the living room, she was fully dressed and her eyes were red. She'd been crying, and Leo had to rein himself back. He wanted to bridge the gap between them, hold her tight and reassure her everything was fine.

But clearly it wasn't. And she'd already told him she wanted space. He had to keep his distance, until she was ready to let him close.

Her eyes brimmed with tears when she saw the hot chocolate.

'Come and sit down.' He patted the sofa beside him. 'Tell me what's wrong.'

'I…' She sat down, as far from him as she was able to get. 'Just don't touch me, Leo.'

Now he was really worried. She didn't want him to touch her. Rose, who was tactile and usually ended up sitting on his lap because sitting next to him wasn't close enough, didn't want him to touch her. So was this the end? Was she telling him it was over?

He masked the fear. Now wasn't the time for demands. He had to put her feelings first. 'Tell me what's wrong,' he said softly.

He'd offered to help. Fix it with her. But Rose wasn't sure it could be fixed.

She cupped her hands round the white porcelain mug, but the heat of the drink couldn't warm her. And even when she took a sip—it was the expensive kind Leo favoured because it was the real stuff, chocolate grated very finely so it just melted into hot milk—the sweetness of the drink didn't give her the usual lift.

Because her world was on the slide. Back into the abyss. She closed her eyes for a moment. 'It's Steve. He's back.'

He frowned. 'Steve?'

Could it be that he didn't know? That Sara hadn't told him? 'The one…' Oh, how blind she'd been, how stupid, to think Steve was The One. Far from it. 'My court case,' she said, hoping he'd understand the shorthand.

'Uh-huh.'

His tone was carefully neutral, and he had his lawyer's face on. Unreadable. She wanted Leo to hold her—hell, she wanted to fling herself in his arms and cry all over him. But then he'd really despise her for being weak. So she'd do this like a lawyer. Like the lawyer she'd never been able to be. Step into his world. Do it all dry and expressionless.

She wasn't going to cry any more.

She'd cried more than enough over Steve the Scumbag. Never, ever again.

'So what happened?' Leo asked.

'I met him at college.'

Met him and fell for him and fell into his bed within a week of meeting him. Oh, God. Just as she'd done with Leo. Well, if you ignored the fact that she'd known and disliked Leo for a good few years beforehand. She was making the same mistake all over again. Hadn't she learned *anything*?

She forced herself to sound calm. Tell him the facts. 'His name was Stefan Mahalski, though everyone called him Steve. He was a couple of years older than I was, in his last year at college when I started. He was a jewellery designer. He was good, too—got a brilliant degree. He worked at a studio for a year or so, then went out on his own. Except he had a few bad breaks. Got let down by customers, people didn't pay him, cheques bounced.' Lies. Every single bit of it, lies. Except the degree. If he'd stayed on the straight and narrow, Steve could have done well.

He'd just chosen not to.

He'd chosen to prey on suckers like Rose, instead.

'By then, I'd graduated and I'd got my part-time job at the museum. It was only temporary, but there was a chance it might be made permanent and I might get more hours. Though it wasn't enough to keep me afloat—I needed another job to make it up to full-time hours. My parents—my brothers, too—said they'd sub me. But I wasn't going to sponge off them. Supporting me through college was enough. I'd make my own way. So I started working at the market, on someone else's stall.' She remembered what Leo had said about making compromises; she needed him to understand that she really loved her job, just as she understood he loved his. 'It was supposed to be just a stop-gap. But I found I really liked it. It was something I'd never even considered as a career move, but it was the perfect job for me. When my friend moved to Australia, I took over her stock and her stall. At the same time, I went permanent at the museum. Still part-time, but I liked having a portfolio career. It suits me, Leo. I get to do a bit of everything.'

He nodded, but said nothing.

If only she could read his eyes. They were too carefully masked. Did he despise her, sympathise, what?

No. Keep feelings out of it. Or she'd never be able to tell him. 'Steve was flat broke. Going under. He asked if I'd rent him a corner of my stall. But he was my boyfriend. My fiancé. We were going to get married—how could I even think about charging him for a corner of my stall? So I put his stuff on there and sold it for him.'

'Just like you do with Sara's.'

What was he saying, that it was wrong to do that, too? 'Sara's different. She's my best friend. And she—she's completely honest. She wouldn't lie or cheat.' She dragged in a breath. 'I sold vintage clothing even then, so Steve didn't ask me to sell the modern stuff he designed—just gave me the pieces that were made from broken vintage jewellery, and reproductions he'd made in more modern material. And the customers loved them.'

Leo's eyes glittered. 'But they weren't reproductions?'

She scowled. She'd made a mistake—a huge mistake—with Steve, but did Leo think she was a total airhead? 'I can tell the difference between reproduction and vintage, thank you very much. They *were* reproductions.'

He lifted a hand as if to reach out and touch her, apologise—then withdrew it again. Because she'd told him she didn't want to be touched? Or because he was disgusted by her, didn't want to touch her?

'But I was stupid. Naïve, if you're being kind. It simply didn't occur to me they might be stolen. Or that the "broken" jewellery was never broken in the first place—that it was a way of laundering pieces that would've been too hot. Break them down, reset the stones, sell. I'd never do anything like that, so I didn't think anyone else would, either.'

'Even though your dad's a lawyer.'

He did despise her, then. Though possibly not as much as she'd despised herself in the lowest days. The days when she'd realised just how naïve and stupid and trusting she'd been. How she'd let herself be blinded by love. 'Yes.' She lifted her chin. 'I handled stolen goods. Sold them. Fenced them, whatever you want to call it. But it *wasn't* done knowingly. I really believed they belonged to Steve, that he'd bought the materials and made them. And if I'd had any idea what he was really doing…I would have stopped him. Just like I'm going to stop him now.' She folded her arms. Well, Leo despised her now. Might as well get the rest of it off her chest, so he knew just what kind of idiot he'd got involved with.

Past tense.

Because he sure as hell wasn't going to want to be with her any more. Not when he heard all this. 'You might as well know the rest of it. Obviously the engagement was over. I wasn't going to marry anyone who'd lied to me like that, used me. Not that I got the chance to tell him. He'd walked out by then. After he'd cleared out our joint bank account, right down to the limit of our overdraft. I couldn't do a thing about it because the money was in joint names. And, yes, I was stupid enough to have a bank account with him in joint names. He was my fiancé. I trusted him.'

'You wouldn't be the first. And it happens with husbands and wives, too,' Leo said dryly.

'It wouldn't have been so bad if he'd just taken my money. But he'd also taken out a second mortgage in my name. I had absolutely no idea. He'd forged my signature on the paperwork, but I couldn't prove it. The financial adviser swore blind I'd been there, signed everything in front of him—even though I'd never seen the man before in my life. And when I saw the paperwork, it looked exactly like my signature.'

Leo's eyes narrowed. 'So the financial adviser was lying? Or Steve had got you to sign a mortgage agreement when you thought it was something else?'

'No. Much, much more humiliating than that.' It still made her want to crawl underneath a table and hide her shame from the world. But she was determined to be honest with Leo. If she wanted his help, she had to tell him the lot. 'One of his friends told me that Steve was seeing someone else. The other woman looked a bit like me—so all she had to do was dress like me, go with Steve to the financial adviser and let Steve do all the talking so the adviser wouldn't be able to tell the difference in our voices. She'd practised my signature. And Steve had access to all the right paperwork, so it was easy to make it look as if I'd been the one at that meeting. As if I'd been the one who signed the agreement.'

Leo looked grim. 'That's fraud. Deception. Didn't you take him to court?'

'I tried. But his lawyer claimed I was trying to weasel out of my agreement and blame it on Steve.'

'You had a witness. Someone who knew what Steve had done.'

'He wouldn't testify.' She shrugged. 'In case some of his own shady deals were exposed, probably.'

Leo's jaw tightened. 'Your lawyer should still have been able to prove the truth.'

'How, when Steve's other girlfriend had conveniently disappeared? We couldn't subpoena her because we didn't know who she was. His friend wouldn't give me any more details. Steve claimed he'd only been seeing me, that he didn't have another woman on the side, but he'd been shocked by the court case and dumped me afterwards because he couldn't cope with all the scandal, and I was clearly out for revenge. A woman spurned, and all that.' She couldn't look at Leo. 'So it was his word against mine. Steve's got an honest face. I fell for it—and unfortunately so did the judge and jury.'

'Rose. That's appalling. That's a travesty of justice. It shouldn't have happened.'

She shrugged. 'Words, words, words.' Bitter ones, too. 'His lawyer was better than mine. Both times.'

'There's more?'

He sounded shocked. Hardly surprising. If she'd heard all this from someone else, she'd have been shocked. Shocked that someone could be so utterly, utterly stupid.

Oh, yes. 'He'd borrowed money from a loan shark. Given my address as his. Defaulted on the payments—and then went to ground so they couldn't find him. So they came and took their money in goods. Added a little bit of a warning by way of interest.'

His eyes narrowed. 'What kind of warning?'

'Broke a few things.' Including one of her ribs. But she wasn't going to tell him that. Bad enough that he thought she was a fool. She didn't want to add wimp to her list of faults.

'Didn't you call the police?'

'With no witnesses, just their word against mine, what could they do?'

'Take fingerprints, for a start.'

'No point when people wear gloves.' Her voice was dry. 'Gloves with knuckledusters.'

He went very still. 'Knuckledusters. Which they used on you?'

She didn't answer. Couldn't, for the bile rising in her throat. She could still remember how much it had hurt when the fists had slammed into her. The shock that someone would actually do that to a woman they didn't even know, that they wouldn't believe her when she told them she had no idea where Steve was, that he'd taken all her money and then some so she didn't have anything to give them.

Leo swore viciously. 'I'll find him. I'll paste him over a square mile of London and scrape him up and hang him out to dry.'

Which was what they'd more or less done to her. 'Violence doesn't solve anything.'

Leo's eyes were hot with anger. 'I know, but it'd make me feel better. Just give him a taste of what he inflicted on you. Make him pay. *Personally*.'

'Drag yourself down to his level and end up on a charge of GBH?' Rose shook her head. 'Bad move. And you definitely wouldn't make QC with a criminal record.'

He took a deep breath. 'OK. Intellectually, I know you're right. But I still want to beat him to a pulp. Because he hurt you, and anyone who hurts you deals with me.'

He was taking her part? She felt the tears gathering in her lower lids. 'You believe me?'

'Of course I believe you! Rose, you trusted him and he got away with...' His fists balled again. 'He took advantage of you. In the worst possible way. He lied and he cheated and he hurt you. Mentally and physically.' His face tightened. 'You should have got me to prosecute. I'd have made sure he didn't get away with it.'

'At the time, you wouldn't even hear my name mentioned. You thought I was guilty of handling stolen goods and a bad influence on Sara,' Rose pointed out.

He went white. 'I was wrong. So very, very wrong, Rose. You're good for her. You've helped her grow up a bit. And I...' He raked a hand through his hair. 'I don't know what to say. I want to hold you, Rose. Hold you and keep you safe. But you've asked me to keep my distance.'

'Because I…' The words almost choked her. 'Because I'll taint you.'

'No way.'

Leo moved towards her, but she held one hand up to restrain him. 'I don't feel clean. Especially now I know he's back.'

'Has he threatened you? Come anywhere near you?'

'No. I…I just saw his name in the paper.' And it had brought all the nightmares back. The gnawing fear. The fear she'd fought so hard—and thought she was beating. Until today.

Leo's eyes blazed. 'I'll find him. And you're staying here with me until I've got him. He's not going to hurt you, Rose. He's not getting within a mile of you. I'll make sure of that. You'll be safe here with me.'

But she'd be smothered. And she'd feel as if she were running away. Too cowardly to stand her ground. 'I don't want to stay here. I have my own space. And he's not going to touch me.'

'Too right, because he's not going to get near enough. But I'd be happier if I knew where you were until he's where he belongs. In a cell.'

'He won't know where I live because I don't live in the same flat any more,' Rose said. 'I moved after… Well. Once I'd cleaned the place up. I couldn't stay there. Not with all the memories. And I didn't stay with Sara, before you ask. I didn't put her and Daisy at risk. I'd never do that.'

'I know. Just as I don't want *you* at risk. Rose, he could still find you. Through the market. All he has to do is charm someone there into telling him where to find you. You said yourself he has an honest face.'

She shivered. 'He won't try to find me.'

'Rose, I understand why you need your own space. You lived with him, I assume?'

She nodded.

'So living with me would be…too much to handle. Like going over old ground. I can see that.'

Well, he would. He was quick enough.

'But I'm not him, Rose. And you can have my guest room. Your own space. Stay as long as you like, no strings.'

His generosity made her heart ache. But she couldn't accept. For one thing, she didn't want to drag him into this whole sorry mess. And for another, staying here—even if she did have her own room—would be too much like living with him. Making the same mistake but with a different man.

'Stay with me, Rose,' he said softly. 'Let me keep you safe.'

'Thank you, but I—I need my own space.' She saw the brief flicker of hurt in his eyes before the lawyer's mask went back on. He thought she was pushing him away. But it wasn't that.

Time to compromise. 'But I would like your help with something else.'

'You've got it,' he said, before she even had a chance to explain what she wanted.

She swallowed the tears. He believed in her that much? How she longed to just lean against him, howl out all the pain and grief and despair. But she couldn't. She couldn't go through with this if she didn't hold herself together. She had to stay aloof.

'The newspaper article—the one where I saw his name. It's a fraud case. There's a woman—a computer dealer—and he's done the same thing to her that he did to me. I need to find her. Warn her what he did to me. Tell her to check everything before it's too late. But when I tried to find out where she lived, the newspaper asked too many questions and the court wouldn't help.'

'I'll make enquiries in court tomorrow,' Leo said. 'I'm owed a few favours. I can get the details without your name being anything to do with it.'

Rose felt her stomach freeze. 'You're owed favours.'

He looked at her, unsmiling. '*Not* what you think. I don't do deals. I do justice.'

She believed him.

'Since you haven't asked,' he added, 'I'll tell you why. I've stopped a couple of people making stupid mistakes, pointed them in the right direction when they were running a case. So they'll help me discreetly, without asking questions. And we're going to nail Steve. Together.'

CHAPTER TWELVE

LORRAINE BURROWS didn't live in the flat above her shop, but by lunchtime the next morning Leo's enquiries had tracked her down to a small, nondescript apartment block a few streets away. He also produced her phone number and her mobile phone number.

'Thank you,' Rose said quietly. 'I'll ring her first.'

Except Lorraine wasn't answering her phone. Rose could understand that. When she'd been in Lorraine's position, she hadn't wanted to talk to anyone, either.

'Ms Burrows, my name's Rose Carter. You don't know me but I know Steve—Stefan Mahalski. And I'd like to help you. Please call me.' Rose left her mobile phone number, but Lorraine didn't return the call.

Two hours later, Rose tried again—this time, Lorraine's mobile. To her relief, Lorraine answered warily. 'Hello?'

'Ms Burrows?'

'I'm not talking to the press.'

'I'm not the—' Too late. The connection had been cut.

Frustrated, Rose tried again, and got the recorded message: 'The mobile phone you are trying to call may be switched off. Please try later.'

OK. Last chance. She sent Lorraine a text. 'Steve did the same thing to me. I can help you. Call me. Please. Rose Carter.'

It was another three hours before Lorraine rang back. Rose, who was halfway through parking her car, nearly missed the call.

She finished parking, switched off the engine and grabbed her phone. 'Hello?'

'Is that Rose Carter?'

A voice she didn't recognise. Female. Please, please let it be Lorraine.

And then she had a seriously nasty thought. If Lorraine was still blinded to Steve—thought he'd been suckered in, too, by his friend—she might have told him about Rose's call. Steve might have heard the message on the answering machine. So this might not be the call she was expecting...

She lifted her chin. She wasn't going to let anyone intimidate her. Not any more. 'Yes. Is that Lorraine Burrows?'

'What do you want from me?' The other woman's voice sounded weary. Miserable. As if she were in a deep, dark pit with no hope of ever getting out, and expected this call to be just more abuse heaped on her head.

Rose knew the feeling only too well. Been there, done that, worn the T-shirt until it had fallen to bits. No, this wasn't a set-up. This was genuine. 'I just need to talk to you,' she said. 'Please. What's happening to you...it happened to me, four years ago. Different business, same thing.'

There was a stunned silence. And then Lorraine whispered. 'Stefan?'

'Steve, as I knew him then. Can we meet somewhere? For a drink or something? Just to talk?'

Lorraine's voice sharpened. 'How do I know this isn't a set-up? That you're not a reporter?'

'Look me up.' Rose's voice was dry. 'Go into the library, look in the local paper archives.' She gave her the date. 'You'll see the reports. Rose Carter, second-hand clothes dealer and museum curator.'

'If—if you're who you say you are, why are you calling me?'

'Because I want to stop him doing it again,' Rose said softly. 'And I want to save you going through everything that happened to me. Because, believe me, what's just happened isn't the worst. Go and look in the library. Make up your own mind—and call me back when you've decided.'

Lorraine called about ten minutes after Leo had dropped in to Rose's flat—supposedly on his way home, although they both knew it wasn't.

'I read the reports.' Lorraine's voice was shaking. 'Can we meet?'

'Where and when?' Rose asked.

Lorraine named a bar not far from where Rose lived.

'OK. I'll see you in half an hour.' When she cut the connection, Leo raised an eyebrow.

'Was that Lorraine?'

'Yes.'

'And she's coming here?'

'No. I'm meeting her in a bar.'

He folded his arms. 'Do you think it's a good idea to meet someone you don't actually know in a bar at this time of night?'

Rose sighed. 'I'm not some fragile little specimen, you know. I've done martial-arts training. I can look after myself.'

'Against thugs with knuckledusters?' Leo's voice was wry. 'Even if you're a fifth dan black belt, I'd still rather you didn't risk it. I'll go with you.'

'She's meeting *me*. If she sees you, it might scare her off.'

He wasn't put off. 'Then I'll sit at a different table. Where I can still see you. Where I can reach you quickly if I need to.'

She rolled her eyes. 'What are you, my minder?'

He shrugged. 'Be as sarcastic as you like. I'm still going with you, Rose. You're not doing it on your own.'

Rose didn't bother to try out-arguing him. She knew he'd win. But she made him keep his promise to sit at a different table in the bar, in exchange for a promise to ask Lorraine if he could join them.

When Lorraine Burrows walked in, a few minutes later, Rose was sitting on her own with a bottle of white wine and two glasses. Rose recognised her from her photograph in the paper; clearly Lorraine did likewise, because she came straight over to Rose's table.

'Thank you for agreeing to meet me,' Rose said, pouring Lorraine a drink. 'Here. And let's drink to Steve getting his just deserts.'

Lorraine left her glass untouched. 'He won't. He's done it to you. He's done it to me. He'll find someone else to take in.'

'Not this time,' Rose said. 'Um, before we start, I should tell you I'm not exactly here on my own.'

Lorraine's eyes widened. 'What?'

'The guy who's with me is a lawyer. And he's on our side.'

'Lawyer?' Lorraine used a very pithy description.

Rose grinned. 'I'd agree with that, in most cases. Though I'd make an exception for my dad and my brother. And Leo.'

'Leo?'

'My…' Her man. Though she wasn't sure if this whole mess would change that. 'My best friend's brother,' she explained, and pointed him out to Lorraine. 'He wouldn't let me come on my own. In case this was some kind of set-up and Steve…' She sucked in a breath. 'I'd better tell you the full story. But I'll warn you, it isn't pleasant.'

Lorraine was silent for a moment, looking torn between staying and running. Finally, she sighed. 'If he's with you and he's a lawyer, then maybe he'd better join us.'

Rose beckoned Leo over and introduced him, then told Lorraine everything she'd told Leo the previous night.

'I know what it's like. How long it takes to scrub the stain from your name. People still doubt me,' Rose said.

Leo's fingers found hers and squeezed hard, a silent signal that he didn't doubt her any more—and he'd defend her to the hilt.

'I feel so stupid,' Lorraine said. 'Forty-two and divorced. I was so flattered when a younger man asked me out. Someone as good-looking as Steve could've had anyone he chose. And he'd picked me. Even though I'm thirteen years older than him.' She gave a wry smile. 'I guess I was a sitting duck.'

'It's the way he operates,' Rose said. 'With me, he picked the quietest first-year student in college, the one who'd be grateful that the coolest student in the art department had asked her out. Too grateful to start asking questions.'

Leo gave her a sidelong look. 'Rose Carter, you've never been quiet in all the years I've known you.'

'He knew me before you did,' she shot back. 'I *was* quiet, when

I first started college. I kept myself to myself, except for Sara. Leo's sister,' she explained to Lorraine. 'And I was flattered that Steve had noticed me. Now, I realise he could I see was vulnerable, that I'd be easy to sucker in. He's probably done the same thing to a number of other women up and down the country, between then and now. I bet we're not the only ones.'

'So how do we stop him?' Lorraine asked.

'I'd advise you to get a good financial person on your side,' Leo said. 'Someone you've not used before, someone who has no connections with Steve. Get a proper credit check done. Instruct your financial adviser to double-check every agreement you've signed since you met Steve. If he's done to you what he did to Rose, the discrepancy will soon show up. Be very, very careful with your home security. And I'll represent you in court.' He took a card from his jacket pocket. 'Give this to your solicitor. Tell him to call my chambers.'

Lorraine frowned. 'But you don't even know me.'

'I know Rose,' Leo said softly. 'And although I'd like to beat Steve to a pulp for what he did to her, this is a better way of getting revenge. Permanently. We'll clear your name. And we'll go after him and make him pay—whoever his team is, they won't beat me in court.'

Rose knew it wasn't a boast. It was a statement of intent. A promise.

And she also knew that he was doing it for her.

'And I'll testify,' she said quietly. 'If it'll strengthen your case, I'll testify to what happened with me.'

After they'd dropped Lorraine back at her flat, Leo took Rose home.

'You're being incredibly brave about this,' he said. 'It can't be easy for you, reliving what you went through.'

'I don't want him to scam anyone else,' Rose said. 'It's the only way.'

'It's still not easy. Especially in court, because you'll be cross-examined and Steve's team will try to discredit you to the jury. If you testify, I might not be able to take the case myself—it'd be a conflict of interest because I'm involved with you—but I can still oversee it. The barrister will use *my* arguments. And I'll be kept informed every step of the way.' He rubbed the tip of his nose against hers. 'It's one of the things I love about you. You're bright and you're hard-working and you're gutsy. I realise now just how much of your life you've had to rebuild, and it hasn't been easy for you at all.'

She went very still. Had he just said the L-word?

His mouth found hers. Briefly. Sweetly. 'I love you, Rose.'

Oh, dear God. He *had* said the L-word. Her pulse accelerated. 'You can't.'

'Too late.' He sat down on her sofa and pulled her onto his lap. 'I've known for a while, actually.' His eyes glittered with amusement. 'Since—ooh—just before you accused me of being like Pavlov's dogs.'

He loved her. And he'd told her when she'd least expected it.

'Leo, I—'

He pressed his forefinger lightly against her mouth. 'Don't say anything. I know you have trust issues—and, after what happened to you, that's not surprising. I understand that. I'm not going to push you. There's plenty of time. And I'm a patient man.'

She scoffed at that. 'Leo Ballantyne, you are so not patient. You expect things done in your way and at your speed. You moan like hell about clerks and judges who witter on.'

He laughed. 'That's different. That's work. This is personal.'

'You don't have any patience with Sara.'

'I do. Well, I'm getting better,' he amended. 'Thanks to you, I actually get on OK with my baby sister nowadays. She says you're a good influence on me. And you've certainly stopped her exaggerating as much as she did.'

Rose had been a bit chary about telling Sara she was seeing Leo, but Sara had taken it surprisingly well, after grumbling that she couldn't ask her best friend for the gory details of her love life any more because it would be just too ewww.

'Rose.' He kissed her lightly again. 'I wish you'd move in with me. So I can keep you safe.'

She shook her head. 'I like having my own space. I'm not going to let Steve and his thuggy friends frighten me out of my home again. I'm staying put. And, no, I'm not letting you move in here, either. It's too small for two.'

'I don't mind being a bit close and personal.'

'Well, I do.' She still hadn't recovered from the fact that he'd used the L-word.

He sighed. 'OK. I won't argue. But I want you to promise me something.'

'What?'

'If you're worried at any time, I want you to call me. Even if it's stupid o'clock in the morning—if you're scared, you ring me.'

'I…'

'Your choice.' His tone was even, but his eyes were deadly serious. 'Promise me, or move in with me.'

Not much of a choice. Either way, it meant she had to rely on him.

As if he'd guessed her fears, he said softly, 'I'll be there for you, Rose. I won't let you down like Steve did. And anyone who lays a finger on you has me to deal with.'

The expression on his face made her think he'd be a formidable opponent. Anywhere. And on his home territory—in court—he'd be seriously scary. 'Violence doesn't solve anything,' she reminded him.

'I know, but there are other ways. Ways we're going to take right now.' He stroked her hair. 'Seeing as you insist on staying in your own space, will you at least let me get some extra security on your flat?'

Her eyes widened. 'You think he might come after me?'

His face was grim. 'Once he realises you're the one stopping him trampling all over Lorraine…' He gave a small shake of his head. 'No, he's probably too much of a coward to do it himself. Even so, I don't want you taking any chances.'

She remembered the night she'd come home to find her flat smashed up. And what had happened afterwards. A shiver ran through her. She really, really didn't want to go through that again. 'OK. We'll do the security bit.'

'Good.' He made a couple of quick phone calls, then smiled

at her. 'Sorted. Let me have your key, and it'll all be done by the end of tomorrow morning.'

She frowned. 'How come you know about this stuff?'

He shrugged. 'Occasionally I've dealt with underworld cases. Gangmaster stuff. What they do is very lucrative, and that sort of person doesn't want to lose what he regards as his rights. Sometimes they try and—' he broke off, as if searching for the right phrase '—intimidate you.'

'You've been threatened?' Her eyes widened. 'People tried to hurt you? Broke into your flat and left you—well—stuff like the horse's head in *The Godfather*?'

His face gave nothing away. 'It's been dealt with. In the past and staying there. It's not a problem.'

Leo Ballantyne could be very, very scary, Rose thought.

And she was very glad he was on her side.

CHAPTER THIRTEEN

ROSE felt safer when Leo's contacts had installed the extra security measures, though she wasn't happy about the fact that they refused payment—Leo had already dealt with it and he refused flatly to let her pay him back.

Everything was fine until her next trip to the Birmingham Rag Market. She'd gone by train, for once; it wasn't a problem until she got back to Camden. And then she noticed something out of the corner of her eye.

Someone staring at her.

She shook herself. Of course that man hadn't been looking at her. She was just being paranoid.

All the same, she was wary. Kept glancing over her shoulder all the way down the road. Jumping at every shadow.

It was just like going back four years. To the days when she'd scrubbed her own blood off her doorframe. The days when she'd hurt every time she breathed, thanks to her broken rib. To the days when it had been an effort to set foot outside her own front door, in case they were waiting for her and the punches and kicks would start again.

She was over that now. Moved out and moved on. She wasn't going to let fear rule her life again. She wasn't going to run.

But she still felt as if someone was watching her. Staring at her.

She glanced round, on the pretext of shifting her bags.

That guy, a few paces behind her—had she seen him before? Hadn't he been on the train? Was he following her?

Ice trickled down her spine. And if he was…what then? What did he want? Was he going to warn her off?

She went into the next shop. Browsed for a good ten minutes. Bought a newspaper. Went back onto the street.

And he was still there.

She swore under her breath and went back into the newsagent's. No way would anyone do anything to her right in the middle of a shop in the middle of the afternoon, would they? She'd be safe here.

So. Call the police? No point. The second a panda car pulled up outside, he'd be gone. And she'd feel as if she were wasting police time, saying that she thought a man might have been following her but she didn't have any proof.

Get a taxi home? No. Because he might follow her—and then he'd know where she lived. Even though Leo had installed extra security, she still had to leave the flat. Go to work tomorrow. And once she was out of her flat…

Her hands balled into fists. How *dared* he try to intimidate her like this? She was tempted, just for a second, to go out there and face him. Put her martial arts training to the test.

Then again, he might not be alone. And Leo was right. She wasn't even a black belt, let alone a fifth dan. She'd be able to fend off one surprise attacker, buy herself enough time to run for it, but that was about all. She wasn't a female Bruce Lee who could spin through the air and knock out all her attackers with a few well-aimed kicks.

Which left her no choice.

She rang Leo's mobile phone. Please, please, please let him be out of court and not in a briefing meeting. Please let him be in an area with a decent signal. Please let him answer. Please.

He did. 'Hi, Rose.'

'Hi. Um, you know that promise I made? Well, it's stupid o'clock in the afternoon.'

He got the message immediately. 'Where are you?'

'In a newsagent's in Camden.' She gave him the address.

'What's happened?'

'I…I think someone's following me. I've been in here for a while—and he's outside. Looking in a shop window. Waiting.'

'Got a description?' Leo asked.

'Yes.'

'Good. Call the police. I'm on my way. And, Rose—stay where you are. Where you're safe.'

By the time the police arrived, the man had gone, and Rose felt stupid. 'I might have imagined it.'

'Not necessarily.' Leo swiftly explained the situation to the constable. 'I know that without any actual threats made, you can't do anything. But I want this reported anyway. It's still evidence. Intimidation of witness. We'll be using this in court.'

So Rose gave the details of the non-incident and a detailed description of the man she thought had been following her. And when Leo called a taxi, he gave directions to go straight to his flat. 'Don't argue, Rose,' he said softly. 'I'm not prepared to compromise your safety. Tell me what you need from your flat, and I'll get it. But you're staying with me now until this is sorted out. I want you to take taxis everywhere when I'm not with you—to the museum, to the market, wherever you need to go.' He scribbled down a number for her. 'I have an account here. Use it.'

Caring for her safety was one thing, but this was taking over on a huge scale. Taking away her independence. 'I'll pay for my own taxis,' she said stiffly.

He took her hand. 'Rose. This is for *my* peace of mind. So it's my bill. And if you argue, I'll set Sara on you. I assume she knows all about the last time?'

'She was the one who drove me to hospital.' The words were out before she realised.

Leo's voice was very, very quiet. 'You didn't say they'd put you in hospital.'

'They didn't, not really. I went to the emergency department. The doctors just checked me over, did an X-ray because of the bruising and gave me painkillers.' She shrugged. 'You can't treat a broken rib. It has to heal by itself. It just hurts for a couple of weeks and then it's OK.'

'Just hurts for a couple of weeks.' A muscle in his jaw flickered. 'It's not going to happen again, Rose. He'll go down, this time. And he won't have an easy time in prison—there's a kind of code of honour there. Those who hurt women or children…' His eyes glittered. 'Let's just say he won't get any sympathy from the other inmates. And it won't take them long to find out what he did.'

It felt odd, giving Leo the key to her flat—even though, strictly, it was for the second time; after her security had been fitted, he'd returned her key without comment.

It felt even odder, being alone in his flat. She couldn't concentrate on a film—his DVDs were nearly all film noir, and she really couldn't handle a suspense movie right now. With Leo beside her telling her when she could uncover her eyes, it was fine. On her own… No. She wasn't in the mood for listening to music, either. And being inside was horrible. She felt trapped. Trapped in a place that wasn't hers.

She realised Leo was protecting her. That he loved her. That he'd be terribly hurt if he knew how out of place she felt in his flat—his personal space. And it wasn't his fault she felt this way—it wasn't his fault at all.

'Rose Carter, you are an ungrateful cow,' she told herself loudly.

But she was still jumpy. Leo had gone to her flat. Supposing someone was lying in wait? Supposing he was hurt? Oh, God, she couldn't bear it if someone hurt him.

That was the moment when she realised that she loved him. When her back was to the wall and she was in danger, he'd been the one she'd called. Not the police. Leo. He'd been the one she'd wanted by her side. Because she trusted him. She loved him.

She'd thought she loved Steve. But that was nothing compared to the way she felt about Leo. It was the difference between a muddy, dried-up puddle and a huge, swooping waterfall. Between grey November skies and the glittering arc of a rainbow. Between bare winter trees and the first new leaves of spring.

Maybe she'd tell him. Tonight.

She was curled up on a chair in his roof garden, reading, when she heard the door close. For one panicky second, the idea shot through her head that it might not be Leo. She couldn't breathe. And then she heard him calling her name.

'Out here,' she called back, hoping that the shaky feeling inside didn't show in her voice.

He came out onto the terrace, scooped her out of the chair, stole her place and settled her on his lap. She leaned her head against his shoulder and slid her arms round his neck.

'Hey.' He dropped a kiss on her hair. 'How are you doing?'

'OK.' Weirdly, she didn't feel trapped any more. Or scared. Not when she was in his arms.

'Your flat was perfectly fine. No sign of any trouble. But I still want you here for a couple of days,' Leo said. 'And I'm sorry I'm bossing you about.'

'It's what you do.'

'To my brothers and sisters, and at work. Not to you. My...' He smiled. 'Whatever you want to call yourself. Partner sounds too businesslike. Girlfriend's... well, a bit teenagery.'

'Lover,' she said thoughtfully.

His arms tightened round her. 'That'll do nicely. Though I might need a practical demonstration, later.' He brushed his mouth against hers. 'So. My spare room is all yours. Want a hand putting your stuff away?'

'I...' Oh, Lord. This was serious. She was moving in with him. Only temporarily, but she was moving in with him. She wasn't sure whether it thrilled her or scared her more. 'No, it's OK. Just let me know what I can use.'

'The whole flat's at your disposal. Actually, you need a key. I'll sort it out.' Another light kiss. 'Go put your stuff away.'

'In your spare room. *My* room,' she clarified.

A corner of his mouth quirked. 'Well, I was rather hoping you might choose to sleep elsewhere. But, yes, it's your room. For as long as you need it.'

I was rather hoping you might choose to sleep elsewhere.

Uh-oh. Seriouser and seriouser. They'd never actually spent the whole night together. She'd always chickened out and sent him home, or called a taxi from his place. Because spending the whole night together was getting way too close to proper relationship territory.

He must have seen the flash of concern in her eyes, because he added softly, 'No pressure. Your choice.'

Which made her feel even worse. He'd already told her he loved her. And she hadn't told him how she felt about him, yet.

Telling him now would feel wrong. As if she were just saying it because he'd rescued her from a nasty situation. Gratitude talking, not her heart.

But she could show him.

'OK. I'll put my things away.'

'Sure. Mind if I carry on with some work?'

She'd taken more than enough of his time today. Calling him out to rescue her in the middle of the afternoon. And then she'd let him go to her flat and get her stuff. More time out of his schedule, when he was busy. He had one hell of a caseload, she knew—because he was good, everyone wanted him to be their brief.

Guilt throbbed through her. 'Sure. Just…pretend I'm not here.'

By the time she'd finished putting her things away and setting her rail up for her stock, rain was pattering against the window. And Rose had a truly, truly naughty thought. It meant distracting Leo from his work…but it was also the best way she knew of telling him something she really needed him to know.

With her body.

He'd made a passing comment about her feather boa. And another, about if she'd whistled he'd be sitting up and begging…

She padded barefoot into the living room. Yep. He was concentrating on his work. Hadn't heard her at all. Good. She returned to her room, undressed in silence, wrapped herself in a crimson feather boa, draped herself on his sofa, and then whistled.

Leo glanced up from his desk, saw what she was wearing, and promptly dropped the book he'd been holding. 'Are you trying to give me a heart attack, or something?'

Not the reaction she'd hoped for. Embarrassed, she muttered, 'Sorry. I'll get dressed.'

His eyes widened. 'No, no, no. Don't you dare. Don't move!' He retrieved his book, shoved a piece of paper in to mark the page, and was at her side in seconds. His hands were actually trembling as he stroked her skin. 'Last time I saw you wearing a feather boa, you had a tiara in your hair.'

She rolled her eyes. 'Well, if you don't tell me all the details, how can I act out your fantasies properly, Mr Ballantyne?'

His eyes widened as he clearly worked out what she was telling him. 'Believe me, Rose,' he said huskily, 'you embody all my fantasies. And if it wasn't raining, I'd be carrying you out onto the roof garden.'

She lifted an eyebrow. 'Who cares about rain? This isn't an original boa.'

He caught her lower lip briefly between his. 'Is that a dare, Rose Carter?'

'Sadly, not.' She smiled, absolutely secure in her conviction. 'You don't do dares.'

'Don't I, now?' He picked her up and headed towards the French doors leading out to the terrace.

'Leo! Your suit's going to get ruined.'

He shrugged and reflected her words back at her. 'It's not a vintage suit. Who cares?'

'I do. I mind. It's good fabric, and it deserves being treated properly.'

'Pedant.' He set her back down on her feet, kicked off his shoes and shucked off his trousers and socks. 'Satisfied now?'

'No. But I hope I'm going to be,' Rose purred.

Colour slashed along his cheekbones, and he hauled her back into his arms. 'Oh, yes. I think I can guarantee that.' He pushed down the door handle with his elbow and carried her out into the rain.

It was a heavy shower, even for September, but it wasn't that cold and Rose simply didn't care that she was getting soaked. The heat in Leo's eyes was more than enough to warm her.

'Christmas and my birthday. All at once. And I'm going to unwrap you,' he murmured. He set her on her feet, and tugged at the end of the feather boa.

She pirouetted, allowing him to pull the garment away from her skin. The logical part of her brain told her that what she was doing was crazy. Making love on a London rooftop. Letting him pull the feather boa away so she was completely naked. Anyone could see them.

Though that wasn't strictly true. Leo's roof terrace wasn't overlooked, and even if it had been the plants on his trellis would have screened them from prying eyes. So they might just as well have been in a deserted spot in the country. Nobody but the two of them. All the same, there was a certain illicit thrill about what they were doing. A thrill he clearly felt, too—the rain had plastered his shirt to his body like a second skin, hiding nothing. His musculature was clearly delineated, the breadth of his shoulders and the narrowness of his hips. And his jersey boxers were plastered to him, too; she could see just how aroused he was, how hard and erect.

And she wanted him. Right now.

'So do I get to unwrap you, too?' she asked.

He blew her a kiss and opened his arms. Let her undo his shirt, strip the wet cotton from his skin. Let her ease his boxer shorts down. And when he was completely naked, he lifted her up, supported her weight partly against the trellis, and drove into her, sheathing his body inside hers with one hot, hard thrust. His mouth seared against hers, wild and demanding, and she kissed him right back, pushing her tongue against his and wrapping her legs tighter round his waist.

She'd never, ever done anything like this before. Making love in a garden in the rain. Tipping her face up to the sky and letting the rain beat down on her skin while her lover thrust into her body. And, somehow, exposing themselves to the elements stripped away another layer between them. So the moment just before Rose climaxed, when she looked into Leo's eyes, she knew exactly what she was reading there. The same thing that was in her own eyes. The same emotion that ran through her.

I love you.

A week later, Leo was sitting at his desk poring over briefs when his head of chambers rapped on the open door and leaned through into Leo's office. 'Leo? You haven't forgotten the charity ball, have you?'

'Charity ball?'

'Two weeks on Saturday.' Timothy Merrick rolled his eyes. 'You *have* forgotten.'

'Slipped my mind,' Leo confessed. 'I've been busy, of late.'

'I know, and we're pleased with your work. Though I'm a bit concerned about the Burrows case you're shoehorning in. You really don't have the capacity.'

'She's a friend of a friend. It's important to me,' Leo said.

Timothy frowned. 'Isn't there a clash of interests?'

'That's why I'm not actually taking it myself,' Leo explained. 'I'm keeping a watching brief. And I'll be advising.'

'Hmm,' Timothy said. 'Don't overdo things. You're looking tired.'

Leo smiled. That was hardly surprising. He hadn't been getting that much sleep since Rose had been sharing his bed. 'Thanks for your concern but I'm fine, Tim. Actually, I've never felt better.' And it was true.

'Hmm,' Timothy said again. 'Just put a note of the ball in your diary. You're hosting a table, remember.'

'Right.' Leo paused. 'I assume it's acceptable for me to bring a guest?'

'Don't see why not. Someone from another chambers?'

No. Someone from another world, Leo thought. But times had changed. It wasn't like the days when Harry had fallen for Natasha. Given the chance to get to know her, people would like her, he was sure—they'd accept her for who she was. 'A friend,' he said with a smile. *Friend*. Hah. She was rather more than that.

'Fine, fine. Just make sure you're there.' Timothy smiled back and ducked out of the room again.

A ball would do Rose good, Leo thought. He'd dance with her, drink champagne with her, and spin her round until she was laughing and the shadows were gone from her eyes. He'd ask her tonight, after dinner.

He was stretched out on the sofa, with Rose sprawled on top of him, listening to one of his favourite pieces of music, eyes closed.

She nestled closer. 'You looked blissed out.'

'Favourite Bach cello suite playing, favourite woman in my arms. Mmm. That's my definition of bliss. The only thing missing perhaps is some chocolate.'

She laughed. 'That can be arranged.'

His arms tightened round her. 'Don't move. I'm comfortable.'

'OK.' She rested her head on his shoulder.

'Rose?'

'Mmm?'

'I need a favour.'

She couldn't remember him asking her for anything before. And he'd done so much for her. Given her a safe place to stay, looked after her, made sure she wasn't hurt. How could she refuse? 'What might that be?'

'I have to go to this charity ball. My firm's a major sponsor and they expect me to go.' He grimaced. 'My head of chambers told me today, I have to host a table.'

'And you want to wear vintage dress? Sure, I can fix that.' She ran her thumb along his lower lip. 'I rather fancy dressing you as an eighteenth-century judge. I won't be able to get originals—apart from anything else, you're a lot taller than the average man would've been in the seventeen hundreds—but I can call in a favour from a friend who works in a wardrobe department and get you a very, very good reproduction.' She grinned. 'And you'll look sexy as hell. I'll enjoy undressing you when you get home. Slowly.'

'Actually, I don't need vintage dress—an ordinary tux will do just fine.' He shifted slightly so he could look into her eyes. 'What I need is a vintage clothes specialist.'

She frowned. 'Why, if you don't need a costume?'

'To accompany me, of course.' He lifted an eyebrow. 'Rose, I'm asking you to go with me.'

'But shouldn't you be going with—' she shook her head '—I dunno, another lawyer?'

'I don't want to go with someone else. I want to go with you.' His eyes were intense, serious. 'Look, I know we've been saying right from the start that we'll just wait and see where this is taking us, that it isn't a relationship. But somewhere along the way it changed. And I'm getting used to the idea of maybe not being single any more. About having a life outside work. About having you around.'

He didn't say it, but she could almost see the word in his eyes. *Permanently.*

'This,' Rose said carefully, 'is starting to get a bit heavy.'

'Will you come to this charity thing with me, or not?'

'I…' She took a deep breath. 'Look, you know I tried to be a lawyer. I failed.'

'You found your vocation elsewhere,' Leo corrected. 'You're not a failure.'

'I won't fit in.'

He smiled. 'You will. You're with me.'

And he fitted in perfectly. Yeah. She could see that. That was what frightened her. Seeing her outside his world was fine: he took her for who she was. Seeing her in his world…that was when the cracks would start to show. When everything would start to go wrong.

He cupped her face in his hands. 'Rose. Stop worrying. It's going to be fine. Lighten up. You might even have fun.'

'Surreal.'

'What?'

'You're the stuffy, repressed barrister. I'm the flaky market stallholder. And *you're* telling *me* I should lighten up and have fun?'

'Stuffy and repressed? Right!' He rolled her off the sofa, pinned her down and started tickling her. 'Take that back, Rose Carter. Or else.'

'Or else, what?'

He found her ticklish spot, and she shrieked. 'OK, OK! I take it back.'

'And you'll come to this thing with me?'

She could only think of one way to distract him. 'I love you.'

He stopped tickling her. Stared. Blinked. 'You what?'

'I said, I love you.'

He shook his head. 'Don't think I heard that properly.'

'I said, I love you.'

Leo bent his head to kiss her. 'Still didn't hear you,' he whispered against her mouth.

Now she knew he was teasing her. 'Liar.'

He wrinkled his nose. 'OK, I admit, I just like hearing you say it.' He tipped his head on one side. 'Just once more? Pretty please?'

Irresistible. He was completely and utterly irresistible. 'I love you, Leo Ballantyne.'

'And you'll go to this thing with me?'

'I'll think about it.'

His mouth quirked. 'Looks as if I'll have to use some persuasion, doesn't it?' He took her hand and kissed the pulse at the base of her wrist. Worked his way up her arm with tiny, nibbling kisses. Tracked up to the sensitive spot at the side of her neck and gently bit her earlobe. 'Come with me, Rose.'

'I'll think about it.'

'Playing hard to get, are we?' He stood up, picked her up in a fireman's lift, and carried her to their bed. Unzipped her dress. Took her clothes off, piece by piece, kissing every inch of skin as he uncovered it. Kissed her all over—except the one place where she really wanted him to kiss her. She really needed to feel his mouth against her sex. She wriggled on the bed, desperate for him to soothe the ache, but he didn't. Every time she thought he was about to bring her the relief she craved, he stopped. Swerved away. Again and again, until she thought she was going to go insane.

Then he breathed on her sex, and she groaned.

'Leo. That's *so* unfair.'

'Uh-huh.' He nuzzled his way along her thigh. 'Come to the charity thing with me.'

A charity do full of lawyers. A place where she really, really wouldn't fit in. 'I'll think about it.'

'So I'm going to have to play *really* dirty, then?' And he did. He stroked her and licked her and teased her until her temperature felt as if it were at boiling point. Every nerve ending in her body was sensitised; every cell in her body was waiting, desperate for him to be inside her.

'Leo. Please,' she begged.

'You know what you have to say.'

'I'm going crazy here. I need…Oh!' She groaned in frustration as his mouth skimmed along her thigh again and deliberately avoided her sex.

'Say it,' Leo demanded, and blew gently on her skin.

She shuddered. 'I love you.'

'Not that. The other thing.'

'I'll think about it.'

He teased her clitoris with the tip of his tongue, until she slid her fingers into her hair and thrust her hips upwards. Then he pulled free and swayed back on his haunches.

She opened her eyes and glared at him. 'This isn't fair.'

'Told you I was going to play dirty.' He pushed one finger inside her.

'Oh. Yes-s-s.' She rocked against him, wanting more.

He removed his hand. 'Yes, you'll come to the charity thing?'

'I hate you.'

'No, you don't.' He pushed back in, then out again. 'Not half an hour ago, you told me you loved me. Several times. And actually, you just said it again a minute ago.'

Rose knew when to give in. 'Yes.'

'Yes, you love me, or yes, you'll go to the charity thing with me?'

'Yes to both.'

With what sounded like a sigh of relief, Leo reached for a condom and rolled it on. 'I love you, Rose Carter. And it's going to get better and better.'

As he entered her Rose sucked in a breath. 'Oh. This is better. *Much* better. I'll try to remember you're always right. And I'm glad I never became a barrister. I'd hate to be against you in court.'

He laughed. 'Oh, I think you'd do all right. You're not so bad at haggling. And anyway, in court I'd be looking at you in your black suit and curled wig and remembering what you look like naked. I'd be putty in your hands.' He leaned forward to kiss her. 'And now you can have your wicked way with me.'

'About time, too.' And then she stopped speaking as he started moving, taking her to the other side of paradise and back.

CHAPTER FOURTEEN

'WE'RE not going,' Leo said when Rose finally finished fixing her make-up and came out of the bathroom.

'What's wrong?' She looked worried. 'Is it the dress?'

She was wearing an original nineteen fifties dress, with a strapless boned bodice and narrow ballerina-length skirt, in black tulle; she'd teamed it with black silk stockings, bright pink high-heeled court shoes, and a flimsy organza wrap in the same shade of pink.

'No. You look absolutely stunning,' he said. 'But I want to go and take it all off you. Very slowly. Until your blood pressure's in the same state as mine.' She was wearing a set of graduated black beads that skimmed her collar-bones, and her hair was up. He couldn't help running his tongue along his lower lip. 'I want to take your hair down, too.'

'If you don't want me to wear it up, I can deal with that pretty quickly.' She lifted her hands to the back of her head.

'No, no, no,' he said rapidly. 'I mean *I* want to take your hair down. In private. Later. And if it stays dry tonight we'll dance in the roof garden when we get home. Just you and me.' Dance, and make love. He moved as closed as he dared to her—if he actually touched her, he knew they wouldn't be going anywhere except their bedroom. 'Rose, you look good enough to eat.'

She gave him a wicked smile. 'So do you.'

A shiver of longing ran down his spine. 'I want to go to bed with you. Right now.'

She shook her head. 'We don't have time.'

He was the one who was supposed to be big on responsibility.

Ha. Right now, Rose was the one keeping him on track. 'I know.' He took her hand. 'Come on. Better go. Taxi's waiting.'

His chambers wouldn't know what had hit them, when he turned up with Rose. She had a liveliness, a vibrancy about her that would put all the other women in the shade. She had a real hourglass figure that made him just want to run his hands down her sides, mould her curves with his fingers. And those pink high-heeled shoes were something else!

Best of all, she was all his.

Funny how she'd been there all the time—for years and years—and he just hadn't seen it before. His sister's flaky best friend, the one he'd told himself for so long that he disliked, was the one that made his life complete. A bad girl who wasn't really bad at all.

He held the door open for her to get in the taxi, then climbed into the other side. She looked nervous, he noticed. Strained. Worried, probably, that she wouldn't fit in. Crazy. Of course she would. If she hadn't hated her course so much, she would have made an excellent solicitor; she was bright, and he thought she understood people well. She'd have been brilliant with clients. And the thorough way she worked on her vintage clothes convinced him that she'd have been just as thorough with legal work. Paid the right amount of attention to detail.

And she'd charm everyone at the ball with her warmth and that slightly kooky streak, he was sure. All she had to do was be herself and she'd have them all spellbound.

But she clearly didn't share his convictions. 'You OK?' he asked softly, taking her hand and squeezing it.

'Mmm.'

About as noncommittal as you could get. 'Can you dance, by the way? I never asked you.'

She shrugged. 'I wouldn't win a ballroom championship, but I won't disgrace you.'

He smiled. 'Honey, you could never disgrace me. You're bright and beautiful—and you're the woman I love. The woman who makes my pulse beat faster with just one look.' He paused. 'The thing is, as I'm hosting a table, I'll have to mingle a bit. If

I had my way, I'd dance with you all night and nobody but you. But I can't.'

'Not a problem.'

Though there was the tiniest wobble in her voice. Clearly she thought he was throwing her to the wolves. A couple of months ago, he wouldn't have noticed; now, he did. And it mattered. He raised her hand to his lips and kissed each knuckle in turn. 'I love you. And I really appreciate you doing this for me.'

'It's OK.'

Though they both knew it wasn't. Tonight was going to be a test. A test of whether his world would accept Rose—and whether she could handle being there.

Leo kept holding Rose's hand all the way to Lincoln's Inn, then helped her out of the taxi.

'It's beautiful,' she said as she stepped through the heavy door of the gatehouse in Chancery Lane and saw the medieval buildings in front of them.

'It's one of the least altered of the four Inns,' Leo told her. 'Though don't wax too lyrical about all the green spaces. They used to execute people on the lawns here during the Reformation.'

No mercy. Rose wondered just how much mercy she'd get from Leo's world tonight. 'So why's it called an inn?'

'In the fourteenth century, it just meant a town house or mansion. In medieval times, barristers would live here as well as work; nowadays, not many do.' He slid his arm round his shoulders and walked further down with her. 'This is the Old Hall.'

'It's lovely.'

'Dickens used it as the setting for *Bleak House*. Know how they got the money to build it, back in the fifteenth century?'

The mischief in his voice intrigued her. 'Tell me.'

'Some of it was from gifts and loans by barristers; but the authorities also increased the fines for barristers who fornicated in chambers.'

Rose glanced at him. 'You're kidding me.'

'Seriously. The fine used to be six shillings and eight pence but, during the building of the Old Hall, it increased to a hundred shillings—as well as twenty shillings "if he shall have her or enjoy her" in the garden or in Chancery Lane.' His arm tightened round her and he whispered in her ear, 'But it'd be worth every penny with you.'

She scoffed. 'A hundred shillings isn't much.'

'Not now. It was, then. Probably equivalent to the best part of two thousand pounds in today's money.' He gave her a sidelong look. 'It'd still be a bargain, with you.'

She remembered what he'd told her about wanting to make love with her on his desk. 'Do you still get fined if you're caught?'

He chuckled. 'Now there's a thought. Want to see my chambers, Ms Carter?'

'I suppose that's slightly more original than asking me if I want to see your etchings,' she said dryly.

He laughed. 'Yeah. And we'll be late if I do what I have in mind. Your dress will be rumpled and everyone will have a pretty good idea of exactly what we've been doing. And I don't want to embarrass you.' His hand slid down to her waist. 'But there's always another time. If you'd like to call on me in chambers for lunch, one day next week...'

'Maybe.' If his world accepted her.

The nearer they got to the entrance, the more Rose felt herself freeze inside. This was crazy. She dealt with all walks of life in her job, from the ordinary person in the street at the market to world-ranking experts at the museum. A bunch of stuffy barristers was nothing to worry about.

But it was the first time she'd actually met any of Leo's friends. Colleagues. Whatever he wanted to call them. And she had no idea what to expect. What they'd expect of her.

Breathe, she told herself, and concentrated on keeping her head held high and her feet firmly on the ground. Tonight definitely wouldn't be a good time to fall flat on her face.

But as she looked round and saw the designer black dresses and the expensively cut tuxedos teamed with handmade shirts and hand-tied bow ties, Rose felt more and more out of place. Her bright pink wrap and pink shoes were completely wrong.

Everyone else was in stolid, dull black. Not even a loud bow tie to liven things up. And why wasn't there at least one woman wearing a scarlet look-at-me dress or bright red high heels? Surely they had enough of black suits in the day job?

But apparently not. They all looked almost identical, and she was the one who stood out—the one who really wanted to hide from all the disapproving eyes. Eyes that judged and found her wanting.

'Rose, this is Mark—one of my colleagues in chambers. Mark, Rose.' Leo introduced her with his most brilliant smile.

'Ah, you must be the girl he's been hiding from us. Charmed.' Mark eyed her outfit; although he didn't say it, Rose could guess what he was thinking. *Oh, dear me, no. Too flamboyant. Not one of us.*

'You're not a barrister, are you?' Mark asked.

Yeah, well, that was obvious, wasn't it?

'Rose is a specialist in vintage clothes,' Leo said. 'Actually, she's a part-time museum curator. A restoration specialist.'

He'd said part-time—but he'd evaded the subject of her market stall, Rose noticed. Why?

Probably because nobody here was going to be able to handle that. There was no cachet attached to a market stall. No snob value.

'Vintage clothes?' Mark asked politely.

'Anything from Regency to the nineteen eighties,' Rose said. 'Though obviously I deal in the latter end of the market.'

Ah, she'd said the words. The two words that would make people round here really uncomfortable. 'Deal' and 'market.'

'Very interesting,' Mark said.

Courteous, but desperate to escape, Rose thought, seeing his eyes.

Two seconds later, Mark added, 'Ah, there's Anthony. Must have a word before he dashes off.'

Coming here was definitely a mistake. She should have cried off at the last minute. Claimed a stomach bug or something.

The same thing happened with everyone Leo introduced her to. The men all seemed slightly nervous of her, and the women gave her top-to-toe appraisals. One or two appeared to be genuinely friendly, but the majority had her pegged as a gold-digger and a tart. It was all too obvious in their faces.

OK. This was just one night. She'd survive it. And then she wouldn't have to mix with them again for a long, long time. If ever. So she smiled. Danced. Was as charming as she could possibly be.

And then she went to the bar to get more champagne. Although she was standing in the queue, minding her own business, the three women in front of her were talking loudly. And she had a nasty feeling that she was meant to overhear their conversation.

'Well, she's not what I expected, for Leo. Not his type at all,' the blonde said.

'All this stuff about vintage clothing. What he means is second-hand things,' added the brunette. 'And how could anyone *possibly* bear to wear second-hand shoes? Even if you actually knew where they came from, it's still…rather…eww. I couldn't do it.'

Rose couldn't see their faces but she could imagine the grimaces. And she could hear the disgust in their voices.

'Of course, you know about the court case,' the third—a dark-haired woman in a dress that was slightly too tight for her—pointed out. 'She was up before the Bench, a few years back. Charged with handling stolen goods.'

Rose felt her jaw tighten. For God's sake, she was completely innocent—and the verdict had been just.

'You know, that's not going to look good for Leo, associating with someone who's been on a stolen goods charge,' the blonde said.

'Was it her only sentence?' the brunette asked.

'She wasn't actually sentenced. Apparently, she got off on a technicality,' Tight Dress said.

She bloody well hadn't, Rose thought angrily. She'd been found not guilty, and it had been a unanimous verdict. As well as being the absolute truth.

'She's kept her nose clean since, but you never know, do you? She might just have been very clever,' Tight Dress added. 'I think she might have something to do with that case he's running right now. The computer dealer who's being done for fraud.'

'In cahoots with her, you think?' the brunette asked.

'Could be.' Tight Dress sighed. 'Poor Leo. He's been suckered in, hasn't he?'

'She's made a good catch there. The best catch in our buildings. She couldn't have picked a higher flyer,' the blonde said.

What? Now they were saying she was a gold-digger and she was only with Leo because of the lifestyle he'd be able to give her? Give me strength, Rose thought, itching to bang their heads together and tell them to get a life and explain she could support herself perfectly adequately, thank you very much. Only the fact that they were Leo's associates—that having a stand-up row with them could make life tough for him—stopped her.

'Mind you,' Tight Dress pointed out, 'he's not done so well lately. He's let himself get distracted by her.' She coughed. 'Well. Those do-me shoes say everything, don't they? Of course he's going to be distracted. What man wouldn't when he's offered it on a plate?'

Rose's fists balled. She was a tart, now, was she? Ha. Thief, gold-digger, tart. What would they come up with next? Junkie? Axe-murderer?

'It's such a shame. I've heard he's not going to live up to his early promise, after all,' the blonde said.

Rose's anger died and she went very, very still. Leo's work was suffering, because of her?

'Runs in the family, apparently. Nobody's ever been able to live up to the old man. His dad was the same. Started off well, but peaked too early,' Tight Dress said.

Rose went cold. Leo had admitted wanting to live up to his grandfather's record. But he hadn't said anything about his father. If Leo's father had been found wanting, had Leo loved his father enough to want to make up for him, too? Was that what drove him to work so hard, made him want to be the best? Shine so brightly that his family would get the glory, too?

'And if he's hanging around with someone like that—well, he's going to crash and burn,' Tight Dress said. 'It'll be a pity. But he won't be the first one whose career's gone down the tubes because he can't keep his trousers zipped.'

'Or gets involved with the wrong sort. Look at Harry. He was going to be such a high flyer—they thought he'd beat Leo's father to getting QC. But he never really made it out of the ranks. He's just plodding along in the second division,' the brunette said.

'I *like* Harry,' the blonde protested.

'He's a sweetie. That's my point. Everyone likes him, but he was never going to get anywhere after he married Natasha. She isn't one of us. He doesn't fit in,' the brunette explained.

'Hmm,' said Tight Dress. 'Isn't he Leo's godfather?'

'So he is. What a coincidence,' said the blonde.

'How sad. Leo's got an example right under his nose, but he's making exactly the same mistake,' Tight Dress said with a sigh. 'Someone really ought to tell him. Before it's too late. It'd be a shame to see all that promise go to waste.'

Ice trickled down Rose's spine. Even if she discounted most of what they were saying as being jealous spite, there was still a nugget of truth in there. Leo's work was important to him. She knew he wanted to get to the top of his profession. And, to get there, he needed a good woman at his side. A woman who fitted into his world. A city girl in a sharp suit.

Rose was a city girl—but she dressed in velvet and slub silk and lace, antique fabrics and vintage accessories. Second-Hand Rose. It was what she did, who she was. Tonight, Leo had been very careful not to mention her market stall—he'd said she was a vintage-clothes specialist and talked more about her work in the museum than anything else. A curator was an acceptable occupation for the girlfriend of a barrister. A little flaky and artsy, definitely not well paid, but the academic side of it scored enough points to make her acceptable. A market stallholder—even if she did work part-time as a curator—just wasn't good enough.

And for being suitable wife material for an up-and-coming QC… Not a chance. Not a snowflake's chance in hell. She had no idea who Natasha was—Leo had never mentioned his godfather or his godfather's wife to Rose—but clearly she hadn't been acceptable to the legal community.

Just as Rose wasn't.

If Leo stayed with her, he'd miss out on all his career dreams.

She'd questioned those dreams, so she knew that he wasn't trying to live up to what other people wanted from him. He wanted it for himself. Not for the power and the glory—Leo wasn't like that—but so he could make a real difference to people's lives. Do the right thing. Make the world a better place.

Ah, hell. She knew what it was like to have your career crash and burn. The struggle over the years to keep her job at the museum. The gossip she'd had to inure herself against. She didn't want that for Leo. Didn't want him to miss his goals. Didn't want him to have to face all the might-have-beens and the regrets.

When it came down to it, Leo would have to choose between his career and Rose. She knew right now if he had to choose, he'd choose her and to hell with the world. He'd already made that clear by bringing her here tonight. Showing his world that he was proud to have her as his partner.

But as the years passed and he saw people overtaking him—people who weren't as good as he was—he'd start to resent her for standing in his way. For the fact that his career was on the slide. For the fact that she'd distracted him from his lifelong goal.

Which meant that she had no choice.

Somehow, Rose managed to get through the rest of the evening. Pinned a smile on her face she definitely didn't feel, chatted to his colleagues, acted as if everything were fine. She even managed to be polite to the three women she'd overheard in the queue. After all, they'd done her a favour. They'd shown her once and for all that she'd never be accepted in Leo's world.

And Leo definitely fitted. He virtually *glowed* in his surroundings. The golden boy. The barrister everyone was tipping for the top. How could she hold him back from reaching his true potential? This was going to break her heart, but she knew what she had to do.

The right thing.

She was quiet in the taxi on the way back to Leo's flat. He didn't seem to notice, to her relief. And when they were finally up in his penthouse, he opened the door to the roof garden. It wasn't raining; just another cool October evening.

'I want to dance with you. Just you and me,' Leo said, and put on one of her favourite compilations of fifties music. Loosened her hair so it fell over her shoulders. And slow-danced with her on the patio, just them and the cool night air and the lights of London.

'Hey. I wouldn't have put this on if I'd known it was going to make you sad,' he said, pulling her closer.

It wasn't the music.

Tonight was going to be goodbye.

So she was going to say goodbye in a very, very special way. Give her heart to him, one last time. She reached up, cupped his face and kissed him. 'I love you, Leo,' she whispered.

'I love you, too.'

With shaking hands, she undid his bow tie. Dropped it on his patio table. His cummerbund followed suit. When she was halfway through unbuttoning his dress shirt, Leo stopped her. Kissed each fingertip in turn. Then swept her up in his arms and carried her to his bedroom.

When he set her on her feet again, Rose carried on where she'd left off. Unbuttoning his shirt, stroking every inch of skin she uncovered, committing the texture of his skin to her memory. Something she could relive in the days to come. Because there wouldn't be anyone else after Leo. Couldn't be. Nobody would ever match up to him—and, although she was a second-hand Rose, she wouldn't settle for second best.

She slid his shirt from his shoulders. Stood on tiptoe so she could kiss her way along his collar-bones. Nuzzled his throat. Took tiny, tiny bites. Stroked her way down his back, over the curve of his buttocks. Lord, he was perfect, all taut muscles and firm skin. He was almost as well toned as an athlete; it was hard to believe his job was mainly sedentary.

He was quivering when she undid the button and zip of his trousers. His hands were in her hair as she worked her way downwards, urging her on. She nuzzled him. Breathed in his clean scent. Teased him with the tip of her tongue until he was gasping. And then she pushed him back onto the bed. Unzipped her dress and let it fall to the floor in a puddle—not how a vintage piece should be cared for, but it didn't matter any more. The only thing that mattered was Leo. And this moment. The last time they'd be together.

'I love you,' she whispered, hoping that the tears didn't show in her voice. That she'd managed to keep them frozen inside.

Then she straddled him.

'All my dreams come true,' Leo whispered.

Hers, too. Except you had to wake up from dreams. Even if you cried to dream again, you still had to wake. Face reality.

And she had to face the future without him.

She leaned down and kissed him; if she let him talk to her for much longer, she wouldn't be able to go through with this. And she *had* to go through with it, for his sake.

She rocked against him, feeling the heat and length and hardness of his cock pressing against her through the soft cotton of her knickers.

He groaned. 'Rose. I need…Oh-ḥ-h.' He closed his eyes and tipped his head back against the pillow. 'To. Be. Inside. You. Now.' Each word was clearly an effort. Clearly she scrambled his brain cells as much as he did hers. On one level, it thrilled her that she could turn his clever mind to mush; on another, it made her weep. Because it was proof that those three witches at the charity do were right. She *was* distracting him. And if she stayed with him, he'd never reach his full potential. Never be the man he was destined to be.

She reached over to the drawer where he kept his condoms and dealt with the little foil packet. Then she slid her hand between their bodies and pulled her knickers aside. Guided him into her.

'Oh, yes-s-s,' Leo sighed.

'I need you, Leo,' she whispered, and bent to kiss him. Nibbled at his lower lip. Teased him until he opened his mouth and let her explore him.

Every kiss, every touch of his lips, made her want to cry. Because this was the last time. The last time she'd feel Leo filling her body. The last time she'd kiss him. The last time his hands would touch her breasts—he'd unclipped her bra and tossed it to one side, and his thumbs were circling her areolae, teasing the hard peaks of her nipples. The last time she'd feel her body tightening round his as she rode him.

The last time they'd look into each other's eyes as they came.

She let herself relax into his arms as the aftershocks gradually faded. She needed him to hold her like this one last time. Protecting. Cherishing.

But after they'd shared a shower and gone back to bed, she didn't sleep. She waited until Leo's breathing was deep and regular, and quietly slid out of the bed without waking him. Gathered her clothes. Changed into a much less ostentatious dress.

Leaving Leo was going to be the hardest thing she'd ever done. Harder even than picking up the pieces after Steve's betrayal. She knew she was doing the right thing—but she could feel her heart breaking as she wrote him a short note. Feel the tears burning silently down her cheeks as she sealed it in an envelope, wrote his name on the front and propped it against his computer.

For a moment, she was tempted to go back to his room. Look at him for one last time. But she knew that, if she did, she wouldn't be able to go through with this. Wouldn't be able to bear walking out of his flat, out of his life.

But she couldn't, just couldn't, see his dreams crash down in a landslide. She had to go. Now. While she still had the strength to put one foot in front of the other.

Quietly, she closed the front door behind her. Walked down to the lobby and called for a taxi. And sat looking out of the back window of the cab as Leo's apartment block grew smaller and smaller.

'Goodbye,' she whispered. And she clenched her hands together hard, willing the tears to stay back. *Goodbye. And I'll love you for the rest of my life.*

CHAPTER FIFTEEN

LEO half woke. Sunday morning. Mmm. A whole Sunday morning with Rose, because she'd called in a favour and a friend was running her stall today. Sunday morning when he'd wake her with kisses, make slow, languorous love with her, then laze around in bed with her, strong coffee, the Sunday papers and a plate of flaky, buttery croissants.

Heaven.

He rolled over to curl round her body, and discovered an empty space.

A cold empty space, which meant she'd been gone some time. Rose wasn't a morning person…so when had she left? Where had she gone?

He jackknifed awake. 'Rose?' he called.

No answer. She wasn't in the shower, either, because he couldn't hear water running or her sweet alto voice humming one of the fifties torch songs she loved so much.

Oh, God. No. Please, please don't let anything have happened to her. Please don't let her ex and his thugs have got to her.

He stifled the panic. Ridiculous. Nobody could have got into the flat without waking him.

Though Rose had clearly managed to leave without waking him.

Maybe she'd had a bad dream in the middle of the night and had got up—then, not wanting to disturb him, had gone to sleep in his spare room. That was more like it. She'd cleared up her dress, he noticed. A mixture of looking after her stuff properly and the fact she knew he hated clutter.

He climbed out of bed; without bothering to pull any clothes on, he went to the door of the spare room and tapped on it, very gently. 'Rose?'

No answer. Which meant she was probably still asleep.

He opened the door just a crack—and realised that the curtains were wide open. He pushed the door open fully. The bed hadn't been slept in; and, although Rose's things were all still there, she wasn't.

'Rose?' he called again.

Still no reply.

No sign of her in the bathroom. Or the kitchen. She might have had the same idea that he'd had about the croissants and gone to the baker's, but somehow he doubted it. He was always awake earlier than she was.

No, something didn't feel right about this. His skin prickled with uneasiness. Where the hell was she?

And then he caught sight of the envelope propped against his computer screen. With his name written across the front, in Rose's neat script.

His chest felt so tight, he couldn't breathe. He ripped open the envelope and unfolded the single sheet of paper.

I realised last night I'm never going to fit into your world. I'll only hold you back. So I have to let you go. I'll get my things picked up later.

I'm sorry.
I love you.
Rose.

Leo banged his fists down onto his desk. What the hell had happened last night? He knew she'd been a bit quiet when they'd got home, and their lovemaking had been more intense than usual. But she'd seemed to enjoy herself at the charity do. He'd seen her talking and laughing. *Sparkling.*

Maybe someone had been jealous of her and tried to put her down. But saying that she was never going to fit in? Crazy. And of course she wasn't going to hold him back.

He needed to find her. The sooner, the better. Tell her that no way was he letting her go. Not now, not ever. He loved her, and that was all that mattered.

Where would she have gone? Back to her flat?

He called her home number. No answer. Just the recorded message telling him that Rose was unavailable right now and to leave a message.

He didn't want to leave a message. He wanted to speak to her. Tell her how much she meant to him. Persuade her to reconsider her crazy, half-baked ideas. They *could* make this work.

OK. Not home. He rang her mobile phone.

'The mobile phone you are calling is switched off,' a neutral voice informed him. Switched off and not through to voicemail. He swore, rang her landline again and waited for the answering machine to kick in. Come on, come on, how long was the message going to take? At last, the long beep. 'Rose, this is Leo. It's not over. It's never going to be over. I love you, and that's not going to change. Not ever. Just call me on my mobile when you get this message and let me know you're OK. That you're safe. I love you. And everything's going to be all right, I promise.'

He tried calling her mobile phone several more times, but there was no response.

Maybe she was at her flat but just hadn't wanted to answer the phone. OK. She could ignore the phone ringing, but she wouldn't be able to ignore him in person.

But when he reached her flat, it was empty, and there was no sign of her car around.

Where the hell was she?

Sara. Maybe she'd gone to Sara. He grabbed his mobile phone and rang his sister's number.

'Come on, come on,' he muttered, drumming his fingers on his knee. 'Just get your lazy backside out of bed and answer the phone.'

At last, the phone was picked up. 'What?' an extremely grumpy voice demanded.

His baby sister wasn't a morning person, either. 'Sara, it's Leo. Is Rose there?'

'Rose? Don't be stupid, she's with you.' Sara's voice faded

as she took in the implications. 'Oh, my God. What do you mean, is Rose here?'

Clearly Rose hadn't gone to her best friend's, then. He raked a hand through his hair. 'Um, she's not with me.'

'Why not? What have you done?'

'Nothing—nothing that I know of, anyway. Someone must have said something to Rose at the do last night and it upset her. She's got it into her head that she'll never fit in with my world. So she's gone.'

'What?' Sara sounded almost as shocked as he felt.

'She left me a note.'

'A note,' Sara clarified. 'Saying she won't fit in.'

'And that's the reason she's left me. It's the most screwed-up, illogical—'

'Actually,' Sara cut in, 'she might have a point. Look at Harry and Tasha.'

'That was years ago.' He groaned. 'Oh, hell. I bet someone told her about that. And she's decided it's a warning. It's a stupid misunderstanding, and I'll personally scalp the people responsible when I find out exactly what happened. But I want her back, Sara. And I'm going through seven kinds of hell, wondering where she is or if Steve's got to her.' He gripped the phone harder. 'I was hoping she might have come to you, because she's not at her place. I've just checked. Her car isn't there. Her mobile phone's switched off, too.'

'Oh, no. You don't think Steve…?'

She couldn't voice the fear, either, and ice trickled down Leo's spine. He was supposed to have been keeping Rose safe. He'd let her down. Right now, she was out there in the big wide world. Unprotected. 'I hope not. But she's vulnerable right now and I need to find her, Sara. Where would she have gone?'

'I don't know.'

'Her parents? Her brothers?'

'I don't know,' Sara said again.

'Give me their numbers. I'll call them.'

She sighed. 'Leo, you barely know any of them. I do. Leave it to me. I'll call them.'

'OK, then let me know if she's there. I'll check the market, see if anyone there knows where she is.'

'We'll find her. Don't worry,' Sara told him.

He laughed softly. 'Hey. That's meant to be me doing the re-assuring. Big brother sorting everything out.'

'Annoying baby sisters can do it, too.'

He paused. 'Yeah. You're not that annoying. You've grown up, Sara. And Daisy's a credit to you.'

Sara snorted. 'Oh, don't get sentimental on me.'

'Seriously. I mean it. And I appreciate you doing something for me. Especially after…well. I've been hard on you, in the past,' he admitted.

'Takes two to be difficult. I shut you all out when I was pregnant with Daisy and you lectured me about dropping out.'

'Only because we were all worried about you, and that's the way our family does things. We nag.'

Sara sighed. 'Yeah. Well…maybe it's time I told you I've been back at college part-time for a while.'

'What?' He'd even discussed it with Rose…and she hadn't said a word. 'Does Rose know?'

'She babysits when I'm at my course. But don't yell at her for not telling you why she was always busy on Wednesday nights,' Sara added swiftly. 'I swore her to secrecy. I didn't want any of you to know until I was absolutely sure it was working out. So you could see I wasn't a failure.'

Leo exhaled sharply. 'Of course you're not a failure. I've seen your jewellery designs—I sneaked a look at them. You're good. And you'll do really well at college. Even if you hate the idea of it, you're a Ballantyne. Which means you can't help doing well.'

'Oh, puh-lease.'

'Deny it if you like. It's still true. Plus, as I said, there's Daisy. She's proof of just how well you're doing.'

'And you've had to practically beg me to let you see her.'

Leo smiled. 'She's worth it. And so are you.' He waited a beat. 'Something else I need you to do for me.'

'What's that?'

'Be our chief bridesmaid. And I want Daisy as our flower girl.'

Sara was silent.

'Sara? Are you still there?'

'I'm just trying to get my head round this. Are you planning to get married to Rose?' She sounded stunned.

'If she'll have me.'

'What about being a QC? You always said you'd never have a serious relationship until you made QC.'

'That was before Rose. Whatever she thinks, I know she'd never hold me back.'

'*She* wouldn't. But there's the people you work with,' Sara pointed out.

Leo said something pithy, and Sara laughed. 'My sentiments exactly, bro. Welcome to the human race.'

'Yeah, yeah. But if Rose rings you, tell her I need to know she's all right. Tell her I love her. Tell her—'

'Tell her,' Sara said with some asperity, 'yourself. When we find her.'

Nobody had seen Rose at the market—and Leo checked with every single stallholder. He was back at his flat, at the point of hacking into the court's database, getting Steve's details and going round there to choke the information out of him person-ally, when his mobile phone rang.

He snatched it up. A glance at the screen told him it wasn't Rose, but it was the next best thing. 'Sara?'

'She's safe.'

Thank God. He sagged back against his chair. 'Where is she?'

Sara coughed. 'I promised not to say.'

'What?' Leo swore. 'What does she think I'm going to do? Beat her senseless like Steve's thugs did?'

'She needs some time on her own.'

Leo's hands were actually shaking; he wasn't sure if it was anger, relief, or both. All he knew was that there was an enormous vacuum in his life without Rose. A hole that could never, ever be filled.

'Did you tell her I love her? That she's got it wrong? That everything's—?'

'Leo,' Sara cut in, 'she needs to work it out for herself. Just give her some space.'

His chest felt so tight, breathing was an effort. 'If she doesn't come back…'

'She will. She has to. She's testifying at the trial in three days' time.'

Three days. He was going to have to wait three days. Be patient. Rose's voice echoed in his head. *Leo Ballantyne, you are* so *not patient.*

It looked as if he was going to have to learn how.

He couldn't concentrate on anything for the rest of Sunday. Monday morning at work was difficult, too, until he had a phone call asking him to take over a case in court. And in the meantime he'd set a trail of enquiries going to find out exactly what had been said to Rose. And by whom.

On Tuesday morning, he called his godfather.

'Harry, it's Leo. Are you free for a drink after work tonight?'

'Is everything all right, Leo?' Harry asked, sounding concerned.

'No,' Leo admitted. 'And you're about the only one I can talk to about this.'

'Sure. I'll ring Tasha and tell her I'll be late home. See you in the Great Hall at, what, six?'

'Um—not the Great Hall.' Leo didn't want people eavesdropping. 'How about that little wine bar on Chancery Lane—Fleet's?'

'That'd be fine.'

'Thanks, Harry.'

Harry was already sitting at a table when Leo arrived, with a bottle of red wine and two glasses in front of him. 'You sounded as if you needed this,' Harry said, pouring a glass of wine for his godson.

'Cheers.' Leo took a sip.

'You look like hell. Problems at work?'

'Yes and no.' Rose's actions had given him an ultimatum: choose her or his job. A choice he didn't want to make. Whatever he chose, he was going to lose. 'Harry, when you met Tasha, did you ever think about leaving the Bar?'

Harry stared at him, looking shocked. 'Is that what you're thinking about doing?'

'I don't know.'

Harry frowned. 'I thought you wanted to be QC, like the old man?'

Leo exhaled sharply. 'I don't know what I want, any more. Well, I do,' he clarified. 'I've met someone. Someone I want to spend the rest of my life with. But she's not going to fit into this world, and she thinks she'll hold me back in my career.'

'Like Tasha did with me, you mean?' Harry asked.

Leo winced. 'Sorry. I'm not being tactful here. And I'm not having a go at Tasha. You know I think a lot of her.'

Harry smiled wryly. 'I also remember what people used to say about her. That a pub musician wasn't the right sort of person for a barrister to settle down with. She didn't dress the right way. Didn't join in with legal shop talk. Her toddler music classes were way, way before their time and everyone said she was a flake.' He paused. 'Pretty much what they're saying about your Rose.'

Leo's eyes widened. 'But—Harry, you hardly ever socialise with people from work. How do you…?'

Harry shrugged. 'You know what the grapevine's like around here. People noticed you weren't working your usual ridiculous hours, and you were seen out with her. Didn't take long to find out that she had a market stall selling second-hand clothes. Or about the court case.'

Leo sighed heavily. 'Which was a complete travesty of justice. Harry, she's not a flake. She's clever and lively and brave—everything I want in a woman. And they're not second-hand clothes as in jumble-sale things, anyway. She specialises in vintage dresses from the fifties to the eighties. And what about her other job at the museum? She's a curator. She writes leaflets for them, for goodness' sake. She restores museum pieces.'

Harry gave him a pitying look. 'The same as Tasha's first-class degree from the Royal Academy of Music and her piano teaching. Irrelevant, where the Inn's concerned. They've already made their judgement.'

'On the basis of rumour, speculation, and without having all the facts.' Leo felt his face tighten. 'It's wrong.'

'It happens.'

How could Harry be so philosophical about it, so sanguine? He'd faced the same choice as Leo. And he'd chosen love over work. Never really fulfilled his potential. How did he live with that?

'You could have made QC,' Leo said softly. 'Dad said out of the two of you, you were always the better lawyer. The best of your generation.'

Harry took a sip of wine. 'Maybe.'

'Wasn't that what you wanted, getting right to the top?'

'I thought so. Once. But being a QC isn't everything.' A soft, sweet smile lit his face. 'I have Tasha. Who's worth much, much more.'

'Do you ever regret it? I don't mean marrying Tasha,' Leo added hastily. 'I mean, not being a QC. Not going as far in your career as you know you could have gone.'

'Once or twice,' Harry admitted. 'When someone was given the cases I should have handled, or was promoted ahead of me. But if my choice had to be between having Tasha and being QC, I made the right choice. Being a high flyer isn't everything. I can still be a good lawyer without being a QC. But I'd only be leading half a life without my wife. I certainly wouldn't be as happy. If I'd chosen the law over her, I would have regretted losing her for the rest of my life.'

Leo knew exactly what he meant. If he lost Rose, he'd regret it for the rest of *his* life.

Harry looked at Leo. 'Your dad thinks you're pushing yourself to make up for the fact he disappointed the old man.'

Leo shook his head. 'Maybe once. But I wanted it for itself. Because I can make a difference.'

'You don't have to be a QC to make a difference,' Harry said.

Didn't he?

Could he really make a difference just as a barrister?

'At the end of the day, it has to be your choice. Only you know how you feel. But think about it. If you can't bear not being at the top of the tree, you'll lose Rose. Because you'll have to fight so hard to get there, it'll come between you both in the end. But if you don't mind not being the highest flyer, you can still have your job as well as Rose. Compromise. Have the love of your life and be a good, solid barrister.'

Good, but not good enough. 'Second division,' Leo said bleakly.

'In whose eyes?' Harry asked softly. 'Not your father's. Not mine. Not in the eyes of anyone who really matters. As for your grandfather…you're not quite a chip off the old block. You're not as hard as he was. I sometimes think your grandmother led a very lonely, cold life. Leo was never really there for her. Or for your father.'

'He always had time for me,' Leo said.

'Because you were bright and he thought you could follow in his footsteps. He never had any time for Sara, did he?'

'No.' Leo flushed as he remembered—he'd thought maybe the old man had been dismissive because Sara was a girl, and Leo the elder had had some very, very old-fashioned ideas. Ideas that the feminist Sara had railed against; they'd clashed badly in her early teens. And their grandfather had certainly never spoiled Sara in the way that Leo spoiled Daisy. Never delighted in the little girl's chatter and her love for all things pink and sparkly.

He hadn't had much time for Leo's younger brothers, either, even though they'd followed the family tradition of going into law. 'He didn't bother much with Joe and Milo, either,' Leo said thoughtfully.

In fact, Leo was probably the only one who had good memories of their grandfather. Did he really want his family to feel that way about him?

'You're the only one who can make the right decision for you,' Harry said. 'But, whatever you choose, you have my support. And Tasha's.' He smiled. 'And that of both your parents, if you ever let them close enough.'

Leo shifted in his seat, feeling uncomfortable. He knew Sara regarded him as stuffy and difficult. But his parents… 'Is that how they see me? Remote? Untouchable?'

'They worry about you, Leo.' Harry topped up their glasses. 'You never tell them anything, except about work.'

He hadn't even told them about Rose. So they'd learned about it over the grapevine. Hell. About the only saving grace was that they knew Rose, through Sara. Though he had no idea what his parents thought about her. Whether they, like his colleagues, would judge her harshly without knowing all the facts.

He hoped they wouldn't.

He sighed heavily. 'I'll talk to them. Explain.'

'Give them a chance. Give yourself a chance, Leo. Be the man you want to be, not the man you think others expect you to be.'

Leo smiled wryly. 'Rose once said something like that to me.'

'Sounds like a very sensible young lady.'

'You'd like her,' Leo said. 'She's like Tasha. She's warm and vibrant and bubbly.'

'And she wore hot-pink shoes to a black-tie do.'

Leo chuckled. 'Oh, dear. The grapevine's gossiping about her shoes?'

'Envy, my dear boy.' Harry smiled at him. 'And they'll find something else to gossip about, soon enough.'

Maybe. And maybe Leo could make the compromise work. With Rose.

He just had to persuade *her*.

CHAPTER SIXTEEN

WAITING wasn't something that came easily to Leo. Once he'd made a decision, he acted. Efficiently and effectively. Waiting— especially on other people's agendas—drove him crazy. And he hated every second of it. Every second he was without Rose felt like days. Dragging on and on and on.

Finally, on Wednesday evening he got the text he'd been waiting for from Sara: *She's home.*

Keep her there. Whatever it takes, just keep her there, he texted back, and straight away called a taxi. Twenty minutes later, he knocked on Rose's door.

Sara opened it, mouthed, 'Good luck,' and left.

'Sara? Who is it?' Rose called from the kitchen.

Leo closed the door behind him. 'Me,' he said simply.

There was a crash from the kitchen, and he charged in. 'What happened?'

'Wasn't expecting you. Dropped the mug,' Rose said economically.

Shards of china were scattered all over the floor. And she had bare feet.

'Stay there. I'll pick it up.'

'My kitchen, my mess. I'll sort it.'

'I'm wearing shoes. You're not.'

Her eyes narrowed. 'Stop bossing me about.'

God, how he wanted to hold her. Kiss all the pain away from her face. She looked like hell. There were huge circles under her eyes and her expression was strained; he guessed that she'd had as little sleep as he'd had since Sunday.

'Rose, let me do this for you. There's no point in letting your feet get cut to ribbons through pride, is there? I'm not taking away your independence. I'm being sensible.'

Her mouth tightened, but eventually she nodded her assent, and he swiftly dealt with the broken pieces of china, wrapping them in newspaper and putting the bundle into the waste-bin.

'So how are you?' Leo asked, when he'd checked there were no remaining slivers she could accidentally stand on.

'Fine, thanks.'

And there was a lie, if he'd ever heard one.

'How about you?' she asked politely.

'I've been in hell. Missing you.'

He didn't know whether to kiss her or strangle her. 'Where did you go?'

'Just away for a few days to clear my head.' For a moment, he thought she was going to leave it at that, but then she relented. 'To my middle brother's. He lives near the sea. I spent my time walking on the beach and thinking.'

About him? He hoped. 'I nearly went crazy without you,' he said softly.

'You'll do fine. I'm not good for you.'

'Far from it,' he told her. 'Since you disappeared, my clerk's threatened to resign and most of the judges on the circuit want to shoot me. I'm a better man when I'm with you, Rose.'

'No.' She shook her head. 'It'll pass. We're doing the right thing.'

'No, we're not. This is your choice, not mine. You didn't even discuss it with me.'

'No point. It's better for both of us.'

'How the hell do you work that out?' he demanded.

'Because I don't fit into your world. Never have, never will.'

Leo shook his head. 'You're making something out of nothing. Rose, to know you is to like you—to love you. The legal world can be stuffy, yes, slow to accept change. Just give people time to get to know you.'

'Time?' she scoffed. 'Yeah, right. Like they did at the ball?

And even *you* were bad, there. You only told them about my museum job. Because the other job wasn't good enough. Which proves you weren't comfortable with our relationship.'

'Then why did I ask you to go with me in the first place? Why did I insist on going public?' Leo asked. When she didn't answer, he said quietly, 'It wasn't that at all.'

'What, then?'

'Rose, they needed time to get to know you. I was trying to buy you time so they'd know you and love you for who you are before they heard the words "market trader"—so you wouldn't have to face any prejudice.'

She wanted to believe him. Really. But the whole thing scared her. She dragged in a breath. 'Look, I didn't tell you this before. When I started studying law...I hated it. And I had a nervous breakdown—it took me a while in therapy to get over it. Even though my dad and my brother are lawyers—well, with them it's different. They're solicitors, work in family law. I knew I didn't want to do that, didn't want the heartstrings cases. I thought I'd enjoy the challenge of contract law. But I hated it, Leo. I hated the arrogance of the other students. I hated the lies people told, the way they trampled over others, the sheer greed.'

'That's why I do what I do. To stop the trampling.'

'You do, Leo. But others don't. Others are still like the students I knew.' She shook her head in disgust. 'They'd take a case even if they thought their client was in the wrong, and go all out to win on a technicality. It's all for show. Scoring points. For most of them, it's the niceties of arguing and proving how clever they are that motivates them. I didn't want to be part of that world then, and I don't now. And especially not after that bloody court case. Steve was as guilty as hell, but he got off. And I'm the one who's left with a stain on my name.'

'Tell me,' he said mildly, 'if I asked you to choose between me and your job, how would you feel?'

Rose stared at him. 'Is that what you think I'm asking you to do?'

'You've said you can't cope with my world. So either I lose the woman I love, or I lose the job I love. Whatever I do, I lose. You've given me an ultimatum.'

'I… No, I'm not giving you an ultimatum.'

'You're not even giving me a choice, Rose,' Leo said softly. 'It's all or nothing. If I told you I loved you but I couldn't cope with the market, so it was over between us, what would you do?'

She bit her lip. 'I… That's not fair.'

'But it's exactly what you've said to me about my job. You're expecting me to accept it without even talking about it. Is that fair?'

'It can't work between us, Leo. As long as we're together, I'm going to drag you down. And you'll come to hate me for holding you back in your career.'

He smiled. 'I could never hate you, Rose.'

She folded her arms and looked him straight in the eye. 'But *I'd* hate me for holding you back. I know what it's like to have a career crash and burn, Leo. I know what it's like to fail, watch everything you worked so hard for turn to dust. To have people turning their back on you and sneering at you and talking about you and despising you. I don't want to put you through that— I'd never be able to forgive myself for ruining your dreams.'

'How do you know you'll hold me back?'

'Isn't it obvious? We've already been through this. Look at Saturday night. I didn't fit in. Don't argue,' she said, lifting a hand to forestall him. 'I don't wear the right clothes, I don't have a re-spectable job—at least, not in your colleagues' eyes—and I've still got a stain on my name. Even though I was innocent, everyone thinks what you used to think—that I had a good lawyer to get me off the hook. There's all this stuff about being innocent until proven guilty, but that doesn't seem to apply in my case. I'm never, ever going to live it down.' She swallowed hard. 'I heard them talking about me on Saturday night. I think I was meant to hear every word they said. They think I'm a criminal.'

'Rose, you're not a criminal. And it's just stupid gossip. Ignore it.'

She shook her head. 'I can't ignore it, Leo. If it was only going to affect me, I wouldn't care. I don't give a damn what people say about me, because *I* know the truth and that's what matters. But it's going to break you, Leo. The stain on my name's going to tarnish you, too. People will associate you with me and it's going to ruin your reputation. You're going to be overlooked because of me—because whoever is up against you for promotion, even though they might not be half as good a lawyer as you are, their partner will fit in and yours won't, so they'll get the promotion instead of you. It's a closed world. And I'm always going to be on the outside—which means you'll be there with me. They'll shut you out.' She dragged in a breath. 'Just like your godfather.'

'Ah. I was wondering when you'd bring that up.'

Her face went white. 'You mean, you…?' Her voice tailed off.

'I know exactly what was said. And by whom.' His jaw tightened. 'I've had a quiet word with them.' Quiet, but definitely not minced. The three women involved had been cringing with embarrassment and shame by the time he'd finished. He was pretty sure they'd never, ever tear someone's character to shreds like that again. 'I set them straight about you. I told them that you were completely honest, that by not bringing the real culprit to justice the system had let you down—very, very badly—and the press had given the wrong impression of you. That if I ever hear another lie being spread about you, they'll find themselves facing a defamation charge. And they won't find anyone prepared to act in their defence.'

Her eyes widened as if she couldn't quite believe that he'd stand up for her like that.

Ha. He was prepared to go a lot further than that. He'd fight dragons for her. And he was going to bring Stefan Mahalski down.

'But none of them knew me. None of them even tried to know me. Why did they say it?'

His smile was mirthless. 'Let's just say that you put a few noses out of joint. People who were a bit upset that you'd been able to do what they hadn't.'

'Oh?'

He winced. 'Don't take that the wrong way. This isn't me saying that I think every woman within a hundred-mile radius worships the ground I walk on. Just that some women have… um…set their cap at me, you might say. Apparently I'm an eligible bachelor.'

'"The best catch in their buildings" is how they put it. And apparently I couldn't have picked a higher flyer,' Rose said bitterly.

He smiled. 'Rose, you're not a gold-digger. You're so bloody independent, you barely even let me buy you a glass of wine.' He couldn't stand being so close to her and not touch her. He'd missed the feel of her skin against his. Missed her scent. Missed her warmth. He reached out, took her hand and squeezed it. 'Ignore them. They just didn't take kindly to the fact I wasn't interested in any of them and used my job as a barrier to keep them off. Especially when you walked into my life and took my heart without even trying.'

'You mean, they were jealous? Of me?' she asked, her voice rich with disbelief.

'You make the room light up when you walk in. Of course they were jealous of you. Think about it. They spend their days in black suits and white shirts. Boring monochrome. Linen and wool. You walk in wearing hot pink shoes and a very, very sexy organza wrap. The men are trying to work out how long it'd take to undress you, and the women all wish they'd had the nerve to wear it or the innate style to think of it.'

'Oh.' She flushed.

He smiled at her. 'I don't know about you, but I'd be more comfortable sitting down. And I'd be a hell of a lot happier with you in my arms.'

She shook her head. 'We can't.'

'Come and sit down,' he said softly, tugging at her hand. 'And let me tell you about Harry.'

Harry.

He's a sweetie... Everyone likes him, but he was never going to get anywhere after he married Natasha. She isn't one of us. He doesn't fit in...Leo's...making exactly the same mistake. The words echoed in Rose's head, but she let Leo lead her into her living room and sat on the sofa next to him.

'Harry is my dad's best friend. They went to law school together, and Harry was the best lawyer of his generation. Dad once said he thought my grandfather would've preferred to have

Harry as his son, but Dad never held it against him. It was just accepted that Harry was a high flyer who'd get to QC at a very young age.'

Like Leo. Oh, God. She could see the parallels now. Those women had been right on the money. Leo *was* making the same mistake as his godfather.

'And one day, Harry walked into a pub and heard a woman singing. He fell in love with her voice. Asked her to have a drink with him when her set was finished. And it was love at first sight for both of them.' Leo shrugged. 'She had a first-class degree from the Royal Academy of Music. She taught the piano. But Harry's colleagues all focused on the fact that she was in a band, sang in a pub. It wasn't…quite respectable. Too boho, back then.'

Like a second-hand clothes dealer was now, Rose thought.

'Tasha held music classes for kids who weren't even at school, in the years when—well—pre-school activity classes were never even heard of. She wore clothes in jewel colours—and outrageous hats. Seriously outrageous hats. She was so far out of their horizons, none of them understood her. They dismissed her as a flake and Harry as a fool.'

With every word, Rose was growing colder and colder. Leo could have been describing their situation. They thought she was a flake and they'd despise Leo for wanting her.

'Harry didn't care what any of them thought. He married Natasha. And he lived happily ever after.'

Nice moral. But he'd forgotten to mention one thing. 'Though he didn't make QC.' Leo's big dream.

'He didn't want to, any more. Because he realised that it wasn't important.' Leo shrugged. 'I had a drink with him on Tuesday night, and he told me that being a high flyer isn't everything. You can still be a good lawyer without being a QC. But he also said, looking back, if he'd chosen the law over my godmother, he would have regretted it for the rest of his life.'

Rose dragged in a breath. 'That was his decision.' It wasn't necessarily the right decision for Leo. He was a different person. Wanted different things, maybe.

'Hers, too. Harry talked to Tasha when he got home, and she

rang me for a little godmotherly chat.' He tipped his head on one side. 'She said she'd always felt guilty that she'd held Harry back. But then she realised that both she and Harry would have been miserable without each other, leading only half a life. And it wasn't that much of a compromise, after all. He married the woman he loved and he still managed to do the job he loved. And he's made a difference to people's lives. Quietly, not flamboy-antly—but he's made a difference. And being QC…it's really not that big a deal.'

'So what are you saying?'

'I'm saying that what you heard on Saturday night was true. Harry's been passed over for promotion. Unfairly so. But if he'd really wanted it, he would've gone for it. He made the right choice for him. The career he loves, the woman he loves, and a rounded life. He doesn't socialise much in the legal world—except with my family, really. He's happy. Tasha's happy.' He raised her hand to his mouth. 'We can be happy, too.'

'But you want to be QC.'

'I still can be. But it's not the be-all and end-all.' He smiled wryly. 'I always thought maybe Harry was secretly disappointed that he'd never fulfilled his true potential. But he made me realise two things. Firstly, he's not disappointed and never has been. And secondly, potential doesn't just mean work. It means your whole life.' He looked her straight in the eye. 'The last three days, I haven't had a whole life. I've been as miserable as hell without you. And if this is what the rest of my life's going to be like…I'd rather leave the Bar. Resign.'

'Resign? But—you've worked so hard to get where you are in your job.'

'I used to think my job was enough. That maybe I'd settle down in a few years, when I was further on in my career. But it isn't anywhere near enough for me, not now I've met you. I want you, Rose. I want you in my life. For always. Like Harry and Tasha. I want a real life. A full life. With you.' He stroked her face. 'And if that means giving up the law—I'll miss it. I'll miss it like hell. But I'd miss you more. So I'll resign if that's what you really want. You come first.'

'You'd give up your job for me?' She couldn't quite take it in.

'I'd lay down my life for you,' he told her. 'Because I love you, Rose. I really love you. It isn't just sex or lust or anything like that—though, I admit, I have a tough time keeping my hands off you and there's a very big part of me that wants to carry you off to your bed right now.' Colour slashed across his cheekbones. 'I love your body and I love your mind. I love who you are. You know that moment in the middle of the afternoon when the whole day seems to dip?'

She nodded.

'I get to that point—and then I know I'm going to see you soon, and it's as if the sun's shining right from inside me. And no matter how bad things get in court—no matter what awful things I hear from witnesses—I know there's a good world outside. A good world, because you're in it. And I can face anything as long as I know I'm coming home to you.'

'To me,' she said softly.

'That's all I want, at the end of the day. To come home to you. My lover, my friend. The one who makes me feel life has a point. The one who's taught me that there's more to life than just my job.'

He'd give up his dreams for her.

Well, if he could be that brave, so could she. 'You don't have to give it up.' She took a deep breath. 'They said on Saturday night that Harry was an example. Maybe they were right. He's an example of how you can have a partner who doesn't fit in, but still do the job you love and do it well. How you can have it all.'

'So you'll compromise with me?'

She nodded. 'I love you. And I've missed you like crazy. When I was walking on the beach. I missed you.' She closed her eyes for a moment. 'I wanted to feel you holding me. Telling me everything was going to be all right. Except it didn't feel as if it would be, ever again.'

'It will be, now,' he promised. He opened his arms to her.

She wrapped her arms around his waist and held on tightly. Leaned her head against his chest. His arms were wrapped just as tightly around her.

And then his mouth was on hers. Kissing her as if his life

depended on it. As if he'd been drowning and she was the one who could save him. He was actually shaking with need.

'Rose, you gave me a bad time,' he said when he finally broke the kiss. 'A really bad time. I was going crazy without you.'

'I'm sorry.'

'I need proof.'

'Proof?'

'Show me,' he said.

She gave the tiniest shake of her head. 'Sorry. Can't.'

'Why not?'

'Wrong room.'

His eyes grew hot, and he scooped her up in his arms. Silk, velvet and all. 'Direct me.'

He knew perfectly well where her bedroom was: but he was giving her the control back. Letting her set the pace. And she loved him for it. 'First door on the right.'

'Uh-huh.' He carried her into her bedroom and set her on her feet. 'Now what?'

'Lie down.'

'OK.' His voice was perfectly steady, but his breathing was noticeably shallower.

She lit the tea-light candle next to her bed, then closed the door to the living room. Put on a CD that he'd introduced her to and she particularly liked. And slowly, slowly, she began to strip.

She shrugged off her jacket—an unstructured cardigan-type affair in crimson velvet. The long matching skirt was next, every movement downwards prompted by a long, legato note on the cello; and then she peeled off her crimson silk strappy top. All the time, she looked at him. She could see his chest rising and falling, his breathing fast and shallow. Desire had turned his eyes that stormy grey that always thrilled her, and she could see colour slashing across his cheekbones as he took in what she was wearing: a black lacy strapless bra, matching knickers, and stockings.

Leo was in as much of a state as she was—maybe even more so.

She took the pins from her hair, let it fall over her shoulders, and he exhaled sharply. 'Rose. You're killing me. You're too far away.'

'You want to touch?'

'Yes.' His voice was a hiss of desire. 'Oh, yes. I want to touch. Taste. Now.' His breath hitched. 'Please.'

She sashayed over towards him. Leaned over and let the ends of her hair tickle his face. He laughed, grabbed her, and pulled her onto the bed.

'Better,' he said when she was lying on top of him. 'Rose, I've missed you.' He buried his face in her shoulder and breathed in. 'I've missed the way you smell. Missed the way you feel in my arms. I haven't felt whole without you.'

Exactly the way she'd felt. From the moment she'd walked out of his flat, she'd felt only half a person. She'd done it for the right reasons—to save his career—but she'd broken her heart in the process.

And now Leo was going to mend it.

His hands skimmed up her spine and dealt with the clasp of her bra. Another barrier removed between them. The next minute or so a blur of need—she wasn't sure which of them ripped off his clothes and the rest of hers, but then they were skin to skin. No more barriers, no more hiding.

Leo gently manoeuvred her onto her back and knelt between her thighs. For a long, long moment he was still, just looking at her. 'You're breathtaking,' he said. 'And I want you so badly, it hurts.'

'Me, too.'

But still he took his time. Caressed every inch of skin until she was burning with need. Kissed his way down her body, paying attention to the undercurves of her breasts, the hollows of her hip-bones. Teasing her, arousing her to the point where she was almost hyperventilating.

And then he finally settled his mouth right where she wanted it. On her sex. Teasing her with his tongue, letting the pressure build and build, and then backing off for just long enough to let her plateau before heating her up again.

Just when she thought she couldn't take any more, he took her over the edge with one last stroke of his tongue.

'Leo. I love you,' she gasped as her release rippled through her. 'I love you.'

It was only when he shifted to hold her close that she realised her face was wet.

'Don't cry, honey. I never want to make you cry.' He wiped away her tears with his thumb and tightened his arms round her.

'They're the right sort of tears,' she told him shakily. 'I love you.'

'I love you, too. The for-ever kind of love.'

This time, when he entered her, she opened her heart to him completely. Let him take her back up the peaks of pleasure—and as she came she felt the same tension shuddering through his body, too.

'I love you, Rose,' he said, holding her close and stroking her hair. 'I love you.'

They lay curled together for a while, sated and drowsy; and then Leo traced the curve of her face with his forefinger. 'We may have a problem.'

'What?'

'We didn't use a condom.'

She'd needed him so much, she hadn't stopped to think. Clearly he'd been in just the same state. She took a deep breath. 'Oh, God.'

'Got a solution to that.'

'What?'

'You can marry me. Just in case we made a baby.'

She shook her head. 'It doesn't work like that any more. Plenty of children are born out of wedlock—and, anyway, just because we took a risk doesn't mean we definitely made a baby.'

'True.' He settled her more comfortably against him. 'I'm afraid you'll have to marry me anyway.'

'Oh? How come?'

'Um.' He rubbed the tip of his nose against hers. 'I have a confession to make. I, um, asked Sara to be our bridesmaid. And Daisy to be our flower girl. If I say that pink and sparkly were mentioned…'

'Hang on. Isn't it traditionally the bride, not the bridegroom, who chooses the colours of the bridesmaids' dresses?'

He coughed. 'You'd gone walkabout. What could I do but step into the breach and act as your substitute?'

'A pink sparkly dress.' She rolled her eyes. 'Am I supposed to wear one, too?'

'To match those hot pink shoes? Maybe.' He laughed. 'Honey, I don't care what you wear, as long as you walk down the aisle. To me.'

She'd done this before. Agreed to marry Steve. Thought the rest of her life was mapped out and happy. How very, very wrong she'd been.

But Leo wasn't Steve. Steve had left her to the less than tender mercies of the loan sharks. Leo wouldn't have got into that kind of mess in the first place—and he certainly wouldn't have left her to deal with it. He'd have protected her. Kept her safe. Made sure that not even a fingertip was laid on her.

The system had let her down when she'd needed it. But that would only change through people like Leo—people who would fight for what was morally right. And so she'd have the courage to walk into court tomorrow. Face Steve. Face the jury. Tell the truth. And she knew it would be heard, this time, because Leo would be right by her side. He wouldn't let justice be miscarried again.

'I love you.' She smiled at him. 'And I reckon we have a wedding to plan. Though your colleagues might have had a point the other week about you slipping, because you've overlooked one teensy detail.'

He tipped his head on one side. 'And what might that be?'

'You haven't actually asked me to marry you.'

His eyes glittered. 'That's easily remedied.' He vaulted out of bed and dropped to one knee. He took her hand, raised it briefly to his lips, and looked her straight in the eye. 'Rose Carter, will you do me the honour of being my wife—my love and my equal partner, for as long as we both shall live?'

There was only one answer to that. An answer she'd be repeating in the future, in front of their family and friends. She smiled. 'I will.'

EPILOGUE

Six months later

LEO waited by the celebrant in the Old Hall of Lincoln's Inn. He couldn't remember the last time he'd felt so nervous. Maybe this was how Rose had felt, when he'd brought her here to the charity do.

Maybe it had been a mistake to book the wedding here. Though it had been Rose's idea. He could understand why, too—she was sending a message to the other members of the Inn, loud and clear, that she was part of Leo's life.

He couldn't stand this. Waiting. So not him.

Five minutes to go.

Would she be early? Would she be traditionally late? Would she have second thoughts and back out?

No. She could walk down the aisle to him with her head held high. The court case was over now—Lorraine had been found innocent, Steve the Scumbag was awaiting being sentenced for fraud, and Rose's name had been cleared once and for all. Timothy Merrick had sent her an enormous bouquet of flowers on the day of the verdict, on behalf of Leo's chambers. And Rose had discovered in the nicest way that times had moved on since Harry and Natasha. People's initial wariness of her had melted as soon as they'd got to know her. In fact, Leo thought, since Rose had been in his life, he'd socialised more with his colleagues than he had in his career to date.

And there was standing room only in the hall; people who hadn't been invited to the reception had turned up anyway, wanting to wish them well. Because Rose, contrary to her expectations, fitted in perfectly.

A flurry in the doorway.

His pulse speeded up.

Natasha, resplendent in one of her outrageous hats, walked in with Leo's mother and Rose's mother. A nod from Rose's mother. And then the music started to herald the bride. A jazzy, piano-based instrumental version of one of her favourite Nat King Cole tracks. '*When I Fall in Love.*'

Yeah. He'd vouch for the for ever part of that.

And finally, the procession he'd been waiting for.

Daisy, first—trust Rose to change the order. Daisy, in a pink and sparkly nineteen-fifties reproduction dress with a full ballerina-length skirt and starched petticoats; holding hands with Sara, in an ivory version of the same dress.

And then his heart missed a beat as he saw Rose walking down the aisle on her father's arm. Her dress was very similar to Sara's—boned strapless bodice, full ballerina-length skirt. Except hers was teamed with a hot-pink organza wrap.

And she was wearing the pink high-heeled shoes.

'Something old, something new, something borrowed, and something…pink,' she mouthed as she reached his side.

'And together, Mrs Ballantyne-to-be,' he whispered back, 'we have the sparkle.'

Chosen by him for business,
taken by him for pleasure…
A classic collection of office romances from
Harlequin Presents, by your favorite authors.

Coming in September:

THE BRAZILIAN BOSS'S
INNOCENT MISTRESS
by Sarah Morgan

Innocent Grace Thacker has ten minutes to persuade
ruthless Brazilian Rafael Cordeiro to help her.
Ten minutes to decide whether to leave and lose—
or settle her debts in his bed!

Also from this miniseries, coming in October:

THE BOSS'S WIFE
FOR A WEEK
by Anne McAllister

www.eHarlequin.com

HP12664

BILLI❁NAIRES' BRIDES

Pregnant by their princes...

Take three incredibly wealthy European princes
and match them with three beautiful, spirited women.
Add large helpings of intense emotion and passionate
attraction. Result: three unexpected pregnancies—and
three possible princesses—if those princes have their way....

Coming in September:

THE GREEK PRINCE'S CHOSEN WIFE
by Sandra Marton

Ivy Madison is pregnant with Prince Damian's baby—
as a surrogate mother! Now Damian won't let Ivy go—after
all, he didn't have the pleasure of taking her to bed before....

Available in August:

THE ITALIAN PRINCE'S PREGNANT BRIDE

Coming in October:

THE SPANISH PRINCE'S VIRGIN BRIDE

REQUEST YOUR FREE BOOKS!

 HARLEQUIN® *Presents* ®

2 FREE NOVELS
PLUS 2
FREE GIFTS!

PASSION GUARANTEED SEDUCTION

The big miniseries from

Bedded by

Forced to bed...then to wed?

Dare you read it?

He's got her firmly in his sights
and she has only one chance
of survival—surrender to his
blackmail...and him...in his bed!

September's arrival:

BLACKMAILED INTO
THE ITALIAN'S BED
by Miranda Lee

Jordan had struggled to forget Gino Bortelli,
but suddenly the arrogant, sexy Italian was back,
and he was determined to have Jordan in his bed again....

Coming in October:

WILLINGLY BEDDED,
FORCIBLY WEDDED
by Melanie Milburne
Book #2673

HP12661